MW01042695

THE LIONESS OF EGYPT

THE LIONESS OF EGYPT

THE SHIFTERS OF AFRICA - BOOK 1

LEIGH ANDERSON
ALICE WILDE

Red Empress Publishing
www.RedEmpressPublishing.com

Copyright © Leigh Anderson
www.LeighAndersonRomance.com

Cover by Cherith Vaughan
CoversbyCherith.com

All rights reserved. No part of this publication may be reproduced, stored
in a retrieval system, or transmitted in any form or by any means,
electronic, mechanical, photocopying, recoding, or otherwise, without the
prior written consent of the author.

ALSO BY ALICE WILDE

The Royal Shifters

Her Betrothal

Her Highlander

Her Viking

Her Warrior

Her Prophecy

Hellfire Academy

Fallen

Broken

Short Contemporary Romance

My Cup of Tea

The queen was dead. Beside me, my younger brother, Ramses, technically a man at eighteen but in many ways still a boy, wept. Our father stood stoically as he buried a wife for the second time. Twenty years ago, he buried my mother as well. I did my best to emulate him, but the pain in my heart threatened to spill over at any moment. Queen Anat had been a good stepmother to me, and an excellent model queen. As my father's first cousin, she had been in my life since I was born and was a fine choice of wife after my mother's sudden death. Anat's death was a surprise as well, and we all felt the pain acutely.

As the nearest female relative, I had been tasked with overseeing Anat's mummification process, as Anat had done for my mother. I had watched as they removed Anat's brain with a hook through her nose and discarded it. Then they took her lungs, liver, stomach, and intestines and put them in canopic jars. I placed the jars into a miniature coffin, which would be buried with Anat along with all of her other possessions. I had then helped wash her body with wine before she was filled with herbs and a drying compound and sewn back up. For the next forty days, she was allowed to mummify while my family observed a public mourning, slathering our faces in mud and wandering the city, beating our chests. But this was not merely for show. Even now, months after her death, the shock of losing her had not worn off. In many ways, I did not know how our family would survive without her.

As the horns sounded, signaling the time for the procession from the palace to Anat's place of burial to begin, my brother stumbled as he tried to take his first step.

"Control yourself!" our father, Pharaoh Bakari, snapped.

"I have him," I said as I wrapped my arm around Ramses's shoulders to support him and protect him from Father's disapproval—as I often did. "Go ahead."

Father grimaced, but he held his head high as he stepped forward, following Anat's coffin, which was being pulled on a sled by eight oxen. The horns of the oxen were rolled in papyrus, as they had already been inspected and approved by the priests as suitable for sacrifice. Anat was preceded by soldiers on horseback, priests burning incense, and musicians of all types. Behind us, dozens of palace slaves followed, carrying all of the items that were to be entombed with Anat for her to take to the afterlife with her. The street was lined with people who threw flower petals and scented herbs onto the road and audibly wept for us all.

It took all day for the procession to travel from the city to the burial site. On the day my father became pharaoh, he began building his pyramid. When my mother died, barely four layers of brick had been laid. The masons and slaves had to quickly build her a mastaba tomb nearby. Even now, the pyramid was only half-built, as my father was a man of barely forty. If he were greatly blessed, he should still have many years left to complete his pyramid. As it was, while it did not yet reach the sky, the lower chambers were complete enough to entomb Anat.

As we approached the pyramid, the bulls were led to a sacrificial platform. Braziers were lit on each corner of the platform and wine was poured over each of the animals as the priests waved incense and chanted prayers. Then, the throats of all eight beasts were slit at once. The blood flowed onto the sand. Later, the oxen would be butchered and the meat distributed among the poor in the city marketplaces.

As we stood before the door to the pyramid, a priest opened Anat's coffin and waved incense over her body while reciting incantations. He then opened her mouth so that she could speak and defend herself during the judgment proceedings in the afterlife. As the priest finished, Father approached the coffin and placed a *Book of the Dead* in her hands so she would not become lost in the underworld. Beside me, my brother fell to his knees and cried. This time, Father did not chastise him. His own eyes watered as he reached out and placed his hand on Anat's forehead and mumbled something to her that no one else could hear.

I wondered when Father had fallen in love with Anat. It seemed rather foolish to me that he should fall in love a second time. It was well known that Father had married my mother for love. She had not been a royal, but the daughter of one of his ministers. The marriage had brought no benefits to the throne save one—me. When my mother died, many people saw it as a chance for Father to correct his one mistake, which he did by marrying within the family, thus securing dynastic rule for another generation. While Father was always courteous to Anat, I hadn't realized until I saw the gentle way he regarded her even in death that he had loved her. What a tragedy to lose two great loves in one life-time. A mistake I was determined not to make. When I married, it would only be to benefit my people. I would not suffer pain when he died. What good is grief? It makes us weak. Is a distraction. How could Father govern the greatest and most powerful country in the world if his heart and thoughts were with the dead? I would never allow myself to be distracted by love.

Father stepped away from Anat's coffin and I pulled my brother to his feet. The priest closed the coffin lid, and one hundred men took the place of the oxen to push and pull the sarcophagus into the pyramid. Behind them, the slaves took all of Anat's possessions into the pyramid to be buried with her. Furniture, jewelry, statues, rugs, clothes, and baskets and baskets of food. After Anat and all of the burial goods were placed inside the burial chamber, the door to her chamber was closed and sealed, never to be opened again.

"**K**ing Zakai will never submit to Egyptian rule, Your Majesty," one of the court ministers said to Father as he sat on his throne.

"He will submit," Father roared. "He will come to Egypt. He will humble himself before me and pay tribute. Or he will die!"

"All-out war with the tribes of central Africa might not be the best course of action, Your Majesty," another minister said, his head bowed. "The distance to march an army there would be insurmountable."

As I stood to one side of the room, I sighed and crossed my arms. For as long as I could remember, Father longed to subdue the African tribes and bring them under Egyptian rule. But he had never succeeded. Since Anat's death, he seemed even more determined to make this foolish dream a reality.

"This is Egypt!" my brother, sitting beside Father where Anat once had, said as forcefully as he could with his high-pitched voice. "We have the most powerful army in all of Africa. The tribes live in straw huts. How can it possibly be so difficult to overpower them?"

"Marching an army across hundreds of miles of desert simply isn't possible," a minister explained. "We could never carry enough water. Many of the men would die of heat stroke. Exhaustion. Exposure. And that's if there isn't a sandstorm, which they would be certain to encounter at some point."

"Then there is the matter of numbers, and style of warfare," another minister said. "They would not meet us in open combat. Once we reach the jungle, the tribes would simply attack from the trees."

"Have they no honor?" Father asked, shaking his head.

I looked away so he could not see my disapproval. Waging war on the tribes was not honorable in the first place. I was not against war in principle. I knew that the majesty and power of Egypt was built by our armies. Our own slaves were the descendants of those we had conquered in battle. But I could not see a benefit to waging war with the tribes. Defeating them would expand our border, certainly, but we already had thousands of miles of desert land we could not use. Any more than a few miles from the Nile River and the land became uninhabitable. The African tribes lined the other side of the desert, along the northern edge of the great African jungle. As far as I was concerned, it was a border they were welcome to. Egypt governed the desert; the tribes governed the jungle. I saw no reason to change this.

"We must find a way to do it," Father said, standing and pointing at his ministers. "Come up with a plan, and do not return to me with excuses."

"Yes, Your Majesty," the ministers said as they bowed and then backed away. My brother squirmed in his seat and clapped his hands, no doubt thinking he and Father had succeeded in taking the next step toward dominating the African continent. But I could see frustration on the ministers' faces, and I felt it as well. I would have to find some way to talk sense into Father when we were alone.

"Next order of business," Father said, standing and motioning toward me. "Sanura, come here."

I bowed and then approached the throne, climbing the three steps to take Father's outstretched hand.

"These months since the death of Queen Anat have been a difficult time for our family, and for all of Egypt," Father said. There were murmurs of agreement throughout the room. "Egypt must have a queen. And I must appoint my heir. If nothing else, the death of Queen Anat should remind us all that none of us can stay in this mortal realm forever—even queens and pharaohs."

"May you live one thousand years!" someone yelled.

"May you live one thousand years!" the rest of the room echoed.

Father raised his hand to silence them. "Only the gods may grant such gifts," he said. Everyone nodded and uttered their agreement. "I have delayed long enough. Today, I announce that my son, Ramses, shall officially take his place as my heir. Behold—the next pharaoh of Egypt!"

"Long live Prince Ramses!" the room said as all in attendance dropped to their knees and bowed in obeisance.

I felt my heart drop into my stomach, but I did my best not to show my disappointment. Of course, I knew that my brother would take precedence. It had been a long time since a daughter had been named an heir to a pharaoh. And then only because there were no sons or nephews to appoint in her stead. But my brother...Well, it was understood that he was different. As a sweet and gentle boy, he had never excelled at his studies or in physical training. He was not a leader, a warrior, or a scholar. His greatest desire in life was to please our father, but he failed in almost every respect.

I, on the other hand, was everything a parent could want in a son or daughter. I was smart, strong, and beautiful. Many people had speculated that even though I had a brother, I would be Father's heir. In the end, however, it appeared that Father could not slight his only son in such a way. Even if appointing me as heir would have been the best choice for Egypt.

Ramses gasped and put his hand to his mouth. "Father!" he said, standing, tears in his eyes. "Do you mean it?"

Father let go of my hand and gripped my brother's shoulders. "Yes, my son," he said. "Over these last few months, I have seen you grow from a boy to a man. And I wish nothing more than to see you follow in my footsteps."

"Thank you, Father!" Ramses said, bowing his head.

"But you will not carry the burden of ruling alone," Father continued, turning back to me and taking my hands in his again. "My daughter, Sanura, your half-sister, shall rule by your side as your wife and your queen."

My stomach tumbled inside of me.

"Long live Princess Sanura!" the room crowed.

I tried to smile, but my lips quavered. It had always been a possibility that my brother and I should marry. Royal families usually intermarried. But such a marriage was typically arranged to keep a family strong and my brother... wasn't. It had been my dream for Father to appoint me as heir, and then I could marry someone who would bring great benefit to the family and to Egypt. Someone with an army, money, or vast tracks of fertile land.

Ramses pushed past Father and wrapped his arms around me. "Oh, Sanura!" he exclaimed. "Isn't this the most wonderful day?"

I couldn't help but smile, genuinely. If my brother was to be pharaoh, who better to be by his side guiding him than me?

"Yes," I said. "It is wonderful."

Father smiled and clapped his hands together. The rest of the room erupted into cheers and applause. Father then stepped toward me and placed a menit necklace around my neck. The heavily beaded necklace with a large bar of gold at the front symbolized Hathor, the goddess of heaven, and queens on earth.

"In the meantime," Father said, once the crowd quieted down, "as I have decided not to remarry, Sanura will also step in as acting queen until my death and she takes her proper place beside her husband and pharaoh."

"Long live Queen Sanura!" the crowd cheered. This time, I nearly cried for joy myself. No longer merely a princess. Not a wife. But a queen in my own right. For now, at least.

The victory was bittersweet, for who could ever rejoice in the loss of two mothers? Though, that is the natural way of things. Parents die, and children take their place. And some of us must make that transition sooner than others.

After the formal audience ended and the ministers had

left and my brother had gone to study with his tutor, I was alone with Father.

"Thank you," I said to him, fingering my exquisite necklace. "You do me a great honor."

"I hope you mean that," Father said as he walked toward one of the windows that overlooked the city below. The sun was setting, painting the sky in fiery orange and purple. Below us, we could hear the din of the people, the barking of dogs, the baying of camels. In the distance, the sharp peaks of the pyramids pointed up to the heavens. "You must know that I did this so you would not just be your brother's wife, but his keeper."

"I know," I said. "And I will do my best by him. And by you. But that is many years away."

Father frowned and placed his hand on mine on the windowsill. "I have outlived two wives. Both of my parents. My brother. Two sisters. And your mothers...I lost count of how many other children did not even take a breath in this life."

I gasped. I had no idea that Mother and Anat had lost children. They never told me. Not that it was something we would have discussed openly. Childbirth—and I suppose child loss—was considered a private affair.

"I'm sorry," I whispered. "But you are a young man. You could take another wife. Have more children."

He shook his head. "I could not risk it."

"Risk what?" I asked.

"Falling in love," he said. "If I loved and lost again, I do not think my heart could bear it."

"I didn't say you had to fall in love," I said. "You don't have to love a woman just because you bed her. Or even because you marry her. It would make sense for you to have a woman for companionship. To strengthen bonds and alliances."

"That is true," Father said. "And I tried that. After your mother died, I swore I would never marry for love again. Anat was the logical choice. But she was also smart. And funny. And a good mother to you and your brother. I couldn't help but love her."

"So, marry a stupid woman," I said. "One with warts and no sense of humor."

Father laughed, a loud bleating laugh that echoed off the walls. It was the first time he had laughed since Anat had died. He wrapped his arms around me and held me tight.

"Oh, my daughter," he sighed. "What have I done? How did I get a girl with such a practical mind? Will you be a better queen with no love in your heart? Will Egypt thrive under your care?"

"I love Ramses," I said.

"As a sister should love her brother," Father said. "But you have no passion for him."

I blushed. I did not want to have this conversation with my father and pulled away from him.

"I will always do what is necessary," I said. "My love for Egypt comes first. I will always do what is right by her."

Father patted my cheek. "That I believe," he said. "I only hope you do right by yourself as well."

With that, he left the room, two servants opening the doors to the throne room as he approached. I turned back and leaned on the windowsill. The sun was nearly set, and stars were starting to shine in the deep blue sky. I placed my hands together and prayed to Sekhmet, the warrior goddess with the head of a lioness.

"Dear Sekhmet," I said, my eyes raised to the night sky.

"Please guide Anat safely through the afterlife. May she stand side by side with Mother. And please guide me as well. Help me do what is best for Egypt and to never put myself first."

I felt a warm breeze brush my shoulders and my skin erupted into gooseflesh. I always felt a presence when I prayed to Sekhmet. It was subtle, but I knew she was there.

"Sanura!" Ramses called out through the open door. "Come eat! I'm starving!"

"Coming!" I said, but I quickly added in a whisper, "And please protect Ramses as well." Then I followed my brother to the dining hall.

2

The short sword fell toward my leg, but I stepped back and swung at my opponent's head, stopping just short of his neck. I thought I had won the match, but he suddenly ducked under my sword and slashed upward, nearly missing my chin.

"Did I call the match?" General Chike asked. More like barked as he stepped back and pointed at me with the tip of his sword.

"No," I said through gritted teeth as I stepped to the side, out of reach from his sword.

"No what?" he asked.

"No, *sir*," I said, flipping my khopesh around with a flick of my wrist and gripping it tightly.

"That's right," General Chike said with a smile, his white teeth gleaming. "In this ring, you are not a queen. You are just fresh meat waiting for a butcher."

I heard laughs and jeers from the crowd around us, but I did my best to block them out. At night, the palace was as quiet and empty as any other private home. But during the day, it was a veritable marketplace of activity. Nobles and ministers coming and going on official business. Priests and priestesses giving and seeking blessings. Friends and extended family stopping by for whatever reason crossed their fancy. Servants and slaves rushing to and fro. Even peasants, coming to petition the pharaoh for mercy or to lodge a formal complaint.

Most of my training sessions with General Chike were held privately, in a small exercise room. But today, we needed a larger space, so we were working in the much more open gymnasium. I also suspected that Chike wanted to test how I performed with distractions.

And I was failing him.

I had to tune everything out. The crowds. My new title. The loss of Anat. The upcoming marriage to my brother.

Once again, I swung the sickle-shaped blade of my khopesh around my wrist, trying to find the balance. The weight of a khopesh, similar to that of an axe but much more elegant, made it excellent for swinging quickly.

Chike was the superior fighter—there was no denying that. He preferred the close combat of the short sword. He loved the control it gave him over his actions and had no qualms about looking deep into the eyes of the person he was killing.

"Begin!" Chike snapped and he lunged, the short sword aimed at my heart.

I leapt back. As a woman, I could never compete with the strength or brute force of a man, especially one trained for war. So, keeping my distance from my opponent was a preservation technique.

With my left hand, I gripped his wrist to deflect the strike, then I swung the khopesh with my right hand downward, aiming for his leg, but it was a feint attack. As he raised his leg to avoid the strike, I flicked the khopesh up, making an arc and quick slice to the back of the head. Had we been in a real battle, I could have taken off the back of his skull. As it was a training, I only hit him with the flat of the blade, but it was still enough to knock his head forward, exposing his neck to me. I swung down and—again, had then been a real battle—could have decapitated him, but I only laid my blade against his skin.

"Do you yield?" I asked.

"How can I yield if I am dead?" he asked, then he laughed as he pulled away and stood up straight. Chike clapped and bowed to me. "Excellent, your highness."

I smiled and bowed to him as well, more than pleased with my progress. The roar of the crowd that had gathered around us, both on the ground and in the gallery levels above, was suddenly made aware to me. I waved to those who had gathered and they cheered louder.

This was why I trained. I never really expected to be in a battle. At most, I might have to defend myself from an assassin. If you were a member of the royal family, someone always wanted you dead. But, I thought it was important for my people to know that I could defend not only myself, but them as well, if necessary. As queen, I was the head of my country's military. Okay. The pharaoh was the head of the military, but my brother had no aptitude for strategy. He was terrible at Senet, a popular board game that also required strategy. He could never plan more than two steps ahead. General Chike knew that with my brother as pharaoh, the real person he would both answer to and take orders from would be me. So, it was important that I have some combat training in order to better defend my country.

"You have improved by leaps and bounds, Your Highness," Chike said as we toweled off and headed to the armory.

"It is only thanks to your excellent training," I said.

"Teaching is easy when the student is as willing to improve as you," he said.

"You still think I need to improve?" I asked.

"Always," he said with a twinkle in his eye. "Never think you are above learning more than you know."

"You sound like Habibah," I said, referring to my academics tutor, who I would be going to visit next.

"There is none wiser than she," Chike said.

As we entered the armory to replace our weapons, an uneasy silence fell over Chike. I could sense that he wanted to say more, but was unsure of how to proceed.

"You were conspicuously absent yesterday when my father was railing at the ministers about subduing the African tribes," I prodded.

"Not too conspicuously I hope," he said.

"Father did not mention it," I said. "But I am sure he could have used your counsel."

Chike shook his head as he picked up a dagger and twirled it through his fingers. "The pharaoh is determined to wage war on the tribes. My words will not dissuade him."

"Where do you think this is coming from?" I asked. "Why is he so insistent on this path? What good will it do?"

"For some men, war is the only way they know how to impose control on the world, and perhaps their own lives," Chike said.

"You think this is because of Anat's death?" I asked.

"It gives him something to do now that she is gone," he said.

"As if running an empire isn't enough," I scoffed.

"Not for your father it isn't," Chike said. "Not for now, at least."

I placed my training khopesh on the rack. "So what can we do?" I asked.

"Delay," Chike said. "Deflect. Misdirect. Eventually, he will work through his grief and may give up on this foolish quest."

I nodded. "I'll do my best."

Chike bowed to me and left the room. I went to my quarters and grabbed my study bag of scrolls, pens, and ink. I opened the cabinet where I safely stored the menit necklace and placed it around my neck. I then headed to the city library to meet Habibah.

The city was alive and vibrant today. The weather was perfect. The sun was shining and it was a warm clear day. A breeze from the Nile kept the city from stagnating—at least at this time of year. In the deepest part of summer, the Nile would sink so low you could practically walk across it, and the stink of dead fish would permeate every nose. But now, it was high and fast, running clean and cool.

The streets were thronged with people and merchants set up stalls and blankets on the ground to hawk their wares wherever they found an empty spot. I slowed my pace as my eyes fell upon some intricate gold beads that would look beautiful woven into a new wig and I accidentally bumped into a girl carrying a basket of eggs, knocking her off her feet and causing many of the eggs to smash to the ground. I immediately bent down to help her.

"I am so sorry," I said as I helped her to her feet and dusted her off.

"Forgive me!" the girl uttered, her eyes downcast but her face streaming with tears. I saw the brand on her shoulder that marked her as a slave.

"No, I was in the wrong," I said as I handed her the basket and picked up the few surviving eggs.

"Never, my lady!" the girl said. "I should have watched where I was going."

"That's enough," I said as I opened my bag. "Let me pay for the eggs so you can get some more."

She shook her head. "It won't matter. He's waiting for me."

"Who is waiting for you?" I asked.

"I'm late," she said and then ran off.

"Wait!" I called as I followed her. I couldn't let her return home to her master without paying for the loss of her eggs. Even a kindly mistress would be displeased with any slave who returned home with no eggs and no money.

"You idiot!" I heard a man yell, followed by a sharp slap. I pushed through the crowd and saw the girl on her backside clutching her cheek at the feet of a well-dressed merchant.

"I'm sorry," the girl said as she trembled before him.

"You will be!" the man yelled as he raised his arm to strike her again. I ran up and grabbed the man's wrist.

"Hold!" I said.

The man looked at me, his eyes wide and his face red. "Just who do you think you are?" he asked. "How dare you interfere with the punishment of my slave."

"How old are you, girl?" I asked her.

"S-s-seventeen," she stammered.

"Seventeen?" I asked, astonished. She looked younger. Too thin. She clearly was not fed well by her master. I squeezed the man's wrist tighter. "You pride yourself on beating a girl, sir?"

The man wrenched his arm out of my grasp and pushed me. "On beating a *slave*," he reiterated. "*My* slave. Now move on and mind your business."

"Actually," I said, crossing my arms, "as queen of Egypt,

all slaves belong to me. You are allowed to keep slaves only with my permission."

"Queen?" the man asked, narrowing his eyes at me. "Queen Anat is dead, or haven't you heard?"

"Perhaps you have not heard that the pharaoh appointed a new queen?" I asked. "His daughter?"

"Oh, the interim queen," he said with a chuckle, but then he stopped and looked at me. His eyes fell on the menit necklace and he broke out into a cold sweat. "Q-Q-Queen Sanura?"

"Indeed," I said.

The man dropped to his knees. "Forgive me, Your Majesty," he said. "I didn't know—"

I ignored him and motioned for the slave girl to follow me. "Come, girl. You are mine now."

"Wait!" the man said. "You can't just st—"

"Just what?" I asked, daring him to call the queen of Egypt a thief.

"She was quite expensive," the merchant said.

"Then perhaps you will treat your investments a bit more kindly in the future," I said and turned my back to him, continuing my walk to the library, my new slave girl at my heels.

"Were you very hurt?" I asked her, slowing my pace as we put a good distance between us and the merchant.

The girl shook her head. "No," she said. "Not this time."

"This time?" I asked. "Did he regularly beat you?"

"Of course," she said, as though it was an expected part of life. And I suppose it was. While it was illegal to kill a slave, there were no laws against physical punishments. Perhaps there should be. Now that I was queen, maybe I would look into ways I could improve life for the slaves of the city. I wasn't against slavery. I knew it had its place. But the way some masters treated their slaves like chattel, even worse than dogs, was appalling.

"Well, that won't happen to you in my household," I said. She didn't respond and walked so quietly I had to look back to make sure she was still following me. She was hesitating, looking back toward her old master.

"Keep up," I said.

"A...are you sure?" she asked. "Are you really the queen?"

"I am," I said. She gasped and fell to her knees, bowing before me. "Stop!" I hissed, gripping her shoulders and pulling her to her feet. She looked up at me for the first time and I was nearly frozen in surprise at her exquisite beauty. She had the brightest green eyes I had ever seen. "Where... where are you from?" I asked her.

She shrugged. I supposed she had been enslaved from childhood, if not birth.

"Where are your parents?" I asked. "Are they owned by that same man?"

"My father was a soldier," she said. "Killed in battle. Mother and I were taken as slaves. She died last year."

"I'm sorry to hear that," I said and she looked at me curiously. What else could I say when it was probably my father's army who destroyed her life. I pressed my lips into a thin smile and resumed my walk to the library, the girl following close behind.

The library of Luxor was the largest and most impressive building in all of Egypt, save the palace and the pyramids. The front of the building was composed completely of marble. It was raised up a dozen steps with a dozen front columns five stories high. Inside, the walls of shelves reached up as tall as ten men, every inch crammed with scrolls and books and other writings from around the world. The library employed no fewer than a hundred librarians and scribes at any given time, and all men and women of learning could be found within its walls. I watched as the slave girl's eyes lit up as she took in the grandeur of the library.

"Can you read?" I asked her.

"Yes, my lady," she said. "Though, not Egyptian. My native language. Persian. My mother taught me."

"My mother taught me to read too," I said.

"Your Highness!" Habibah called out as she crossed the floor toward me, her arms outstretched. Habibah was a woman of late middle age, which showed only in the round-ness of her form and the few lines around her eyes. I had no idea if her hair was black or white as she always wore a deep red shawl around her head. "Or should I say, Your Majesty?" She gave an exaggerated bow that made me blush.

"It will always be Sanura to you, teacher," I said, grip-ping her hands tightly.

"And who is this?" she asked, turning to the slave girl.

"A new acquisition," I said. "I took her from an abusive master."

"How benevolent," Habibah said. "And her name?"

I blushed and my stomach flipped in embarrassment. I hadn't thought to ask the girl's name. "Umm...Her name..."

"Keket," the girl said with a curtsey, casting her eyes to the floor.

"Yes," I said. "Keket. Isn't she lovely?"

Habibah reached out with her finger and lifted Keket's

chin, looking into her eyes. "Quite," she said. "Where are you from?"

"I don't know, my lady," Keket said.

"She speaks and reads Persian," I said. "That could give you some clue."

"She reads?" Habibah asked in surprise. "I daresay she might find some interesting things to read on the third floor. Would you like that, Keket?"

"Very much so, my lady," Keket said.

"With eyes like that, I'm almost certain you are Pashtun," Habibah said. "Does that sound familiar to you?"

"I...I don't know, my lady," Keket said, pulling away and dropping her eyes again.

"Hmm." Habibah folded her hands in front of her. "Well, I suppose that is a mystery for another day. Why don't you explore the library a bit while Queen Sanura and I talk."

"Yes, ma'am," Keket said as she backed away, bowing all the way. "Thank you, my lady."

"What do you think?" I asked Habibah once Keket was out of earshot.

"Keep an eye on her," Habibah said. "Pashtun are a very secretive people. They keep to themselves and don't share their traditions with outsiders."

"How do you think she came to be here?" I asked. "Has Father ever waged war with the Pashtun?"

"That is farther east than our armies have ever traveled," Habibah said. "No, she was probably traded from hand to hand across the desert until she ended up here. A hard upbringing to be sure."

"Can I trust her?" I asked. "I was hoping to have her assigned to my personal household."

"As much as you can trust anyone you've just met,"

Habibah said, meaning not at all. "But that doesn't mean you can't take her under your wing. Who knows. She might prove to be a faithful companion."

I nodded and then moved on to more pressing matters. We walked through the library, toward a row of tables. "I wanted to ask you about deflection. Misdirection."

"Oh?" Habibah asked, raising an eyebrow.

"Yes," I said. "You see, the pharaoh—"

A scream rent the air, followed by a ferocious roar.

"By the gods?" Habibah gasped as we both looked right and left, trying to discern where the echoing sounds were coming from. I then saw Keket running toward me, terror on her face.

"Lion!" she screamed. At first, I thought she must be mad. A lion in the library? But then, just behind her, I saw him. A full-grown male lion with a large mane, running toward her, teeth barred and claws extended.

I didn't even think. I jumped up on the table next to me and leapt behind Keket as she passed, foolishly putting myself between her and the lion. I reached for my belt, but of course, I did not have a weapon on me. Who expects to run into a lion in the library? But I could still fight in other ways.

I dropped to one side and swung my right leg in the air, connecting my foot with the lion's nose. The lion stumbled and let out what sounded like a whine. It stepped back and shook its head from the shock. When it recovered, it looked at me with something like...recognition. Like reason. As though I was looking into the eyes of a man and not a beast.

I jumped to my feet and held my hands in front of me. "Easy, boy," I said gently. "You don't want to hurt anyone today."

The lion's eyes then returned to those of a wild beast. He

snarled and let out a fearsome growl, one loud enough to shake the walls and send the people into a panic again. But the lion did not attack me. He turned away and lunged at someone else before I could stop him. The man dodged the attack, and the lion kept running. It ran to the front door, but the door was shut. It raised a paw to the handle, as though he was trying to open it. I realized that the lion wasn't trying to hurt anyone. It was trying to escape.

"What are you doing?" Habibah called out to me as I took off for the door. "The people!"

I knew what she meant. The city was teeming with people. If the lion were let loose...But the lion was already loose here in the library and it hadn't hurt anyone. It just wanted to escape. The library was on the edge of the city. If the lion went out the front door and headed toward the river, he could get away without being taken down by the city guards.

The only problem was that the lion was between me and the door. I slowed as I approached him, my hands open in surrender. "Hey, hush now," I said, looking into his eyes. "I'm not going to hurt you."

The lion snarled and began to circle around me, away from the door.

"That's right," I said as I circled as well. Finally, the door was behind me. I flipped the handle and pushed the door open. The lion barely thought twice before bounding past me and down the stairs of the library. Dozens of screams erupted as the people on the street saw the lion emerge. Thankfully, though, the lion turned away from them and headed toward the river and out of the city, as if he knew exactly where to go.

I shook my head in dumbfounded relief. What just happened? How could there have been a lion in the library?

But before I could make sense of any of it, an old woman approached me.

"You just faced down a lion!" she exclaimed.

"What?" I asked, still confused over the whole thing. "No...I...Well...Maybe?"

An old priest came up next to her. "Truly, you are the goddess Sekhmet come to life!" he said, holding up his hands and looking to heaven.

"No," I said. "I was just protecting my friend."

"Long live Queen Sanura!" someone shouted.

"Praise be to Sekhmet!" someone else said.

A crowd started to form around me of people trying to touch me. Others dropped to their knees and bowed to me.

I looked back into the library and Habibah came to my side.

"Truly, the pharaoh has done the right thing in appointing Sanura as our new queen," she said, which led to more cheering.

"I thought you were coming to help me," I said to her through gritted teeth.

"As long as you have the love of the people," Habibah replied, "you'll never have to worry a day in your life." She then raised her voice to the people. "Long live Queen Sanura!"

"Long live the queen who faced a lion!" they replied.

3

"The Lioness of Egypt," Father said with a chuckle. "That's what they are calling you."

We were in the throne room. Father was pacing, trying to wrap his head around the story that had just been related to him by one of the ministers who had been standing outside the library and had seen the lion run away as well as the reaction of the crowd. There were several people present, all trying to hear the tale. Keket was standing to the side, near a doorway, unsure of what to do with herself. She looked as though she might flee at the slightest provocation.

I blushed and shook my head. "I just did what anyone would have done."

"Are you joking?" Father asked, running his hand over his smooth, shaved head. "Not just anyone would have stared down a lion. No one else did! What were you thinking? Did you know that the beast killed Psamtic, the scholar? It could have been you."

"That's what I mean," I said. "Okay, not anyone would have done that. But I didn't even think about it. I just reacted. I had to protect Habibah and the other people."

"What about you?" he asked. "I just made you queen. What would I have done if something had happened to you?"

"As if losing Mother wasn't enough!" my brother finally snapped, tears welling in his eyes.

"Don't," I said to him, sending him a warning glare to keep his emotions in check in front of the ministers, and especially Father. He cleared his throat and looked away, chewing on his thumbnail. I turned back to Father. "This has nothing to do with Mother. I did it *because* you made me queen. My first thought is for my people. My last thought is for myself."

At that, Ramses jumped from his throne and rushed out of the room, nearly trampling over Keket in the process. Father shook his head in disappointment before turning back to me.

"Very well, Lioness of Egypt," Father said. "I will give you this task: find a way to make war and subdue the African tribes."

"No!" I said without thinking and I heard the room gasp. Father's eyes went wide with shock and rage. "I mean..." I stumbled, trying to correct course. Even I could not openly defy the pharaoh. "I am not well-versed in military strategy. And there are other things we should focus on right now." *Redirect. Distract. Misdirection.*

"Like what?" Father asked.

"City security," I said. "How did a lion get into the library in the first place? What's to keep one from invading the palace next?"

"An anomaly, I'm sure," Father said. "But I will have the city guards investigate the matter. That is not our concern. Our concern is the safety of the entire country."

"Waging war will not keep our people safe," I said. "It will deplete our armies. Leave us vulnerable."

"We need the resources the African tribes have access to," Father said. "The timber. The gold. The slaves."

"We can get them through other measures," I said. "Diplomatic relations—"

"Diplomacy with the beasts of the wild?" he snapped.

I gasped. "Father!" I said. "The tribes are not beasts. How can you speak so lowly of them? They are proud people with ancient traditions, just like us."

"They are nothing compared to us," Father hissed. I was losing my patience. This was not my father, not the man I knew. My father taught me to respect all people in order to gain respect in return. I didn't know what was wrong with him, but I wasn't going to continue the argument in public.

I nodded and bowed. "I will work with Habibah and General Chike," I said. "We will try to come up with a solution to this problem that will be to your satisfaction."

"Good," he said. "Now go, all of you."

The room quickly cleared out and I went to Keket.

"I'm sorry about the awkward homecoming," I said.

"No need to apologize, my lady," she said. "You saved my life today. Twice."

I shook my head. "I'd rather forget about it at this point." I waved the head of the palace staff over to me and he bowed as he approached. "This is Keket," I explained. "I would like her to be assigned to my household."

"Yes, Your Majesty," he said. "Follow me, girl."

She hesitated, but I rubbed her arm reassuringly. "It will be alright," I said. "He will show you your room, get you some clean clothes and a meal, and then explain your duties to you."

She gave an unsure nod, but then smiled as she turned away to follow the servant.

"Oh, Keket," I called after her. "Were you able to find any reading material in Persian?" After the encounter with the lion, I had retreated back into the library until the crowd died down and spoke further with Habibah. Keket was reluctant to leave my side, but she did wander off a few times.

Her eyes lit up and she smiled. "I did, my lady," she said. "Thank you."

I nodded and motioned for her to be on her way. I watched her go and then decided to go see Ramses. He was clearly upset by my actions, and possibly something else. I knew he wouldn't be able to sleep if he was stressed, and if he didn't sleep would become quite irritable the next day, which would make life difficult for everyone. As I raised my hand to knock on his door, I heard a crash from inside. I opened the door without announcing myself and saw that a desk had been overturned, and papers and ink had spilled across the floor. My brother was pacing, his hands clenched into the fists at his sides.

"Ramses!" I yelled, stepping into the room and closing the door behind me. "What are you doing?"

"Go away!" he yelled back. "I don't want to see you!"

"We need to clean this up," I said. "If Father hears of you throwing a fit he will be greatly displeased."

"You don't care about Father," Ramses spat, flinging himself onto the bed. "You don't care about me!"

I took a deep breath to calm myself so I would not lose my temper. Ramses could be exhausting, but mentally he was just a boy, and becoming angry with him helped no one.

"That is not true," I said. "I love you more than anything."

"Not more than Egypt," he grumbled, looking away from me.

"No," I admitted, walking to the bed and sitting beside him. "Not more than Egypt. And you should love Egypt above all others too."

"No!" he said. "I'll never love anything or anyone more than I love you."

"Then it is a good thing you are not pharaoh yet," I said. "You still have much to learn."

Ramses punched his pillow. "You always think you know more than me!"

"I am older," I said.

"So?" Ramses asked, looking at me. "I am going to be pharaoh. Not you. If Father tasked me with fighting the African tribes, I would do it."

I felt the hairs on the back of my neck stand on end in warning. I knew my brother had been heartbroken since Anat had died. One minute he would be in tears, and the next he would be smashing a vase. I had tried to ignore the outbursts as much as possible, chalking them up to a child mourning his mother. But I hadn't considered he might use his rage to wage war on another country. If Father learned that Ramses was willing to launch the war that I was not, he might very well take Ramses up on the offer.

"Ramses," I said as I reached over and stroked his cheek, I could feel the heat of his rage under my fingers. "You are going to be an excellent pharaoh. And one way you are going to do that is by keeping the peace as much as possible. War hurts everyone and should only ever be a last resort."

"That's not what Father says," Ramses objected.

"Father is still mourning Anat," I said, not bringing attention to the fact that he was as well. "He doesn't know how to channel his pain, so he is lashing out at the tribes."

"What about you?" Ramses asked, sitting up and wiping his face. "You aren't angry like Father and me. Don't you miss Mother?"

"More than anything," I said. "Anat was my mother too. She had been my aunt when my own mother had been alive, and I was so young when Mother died, I barely remember her. Losing Anat was like losing a part of myself."

"Then why aren't you sad?" Ramses asked. "Or angry? Don't you want to curse the gods and throw the whole city into the sea?"

"And what good would that do?" I asked. "Invoking the wrath of the gods would be dangerous. And if I pitched the city into the sea, how would I be queen?" I chuckled and Ramses followed suit.

"I suppose you might be a good queen," he said. "But I will still be pharaoh."

"Of course you will," I said, kissing his head tenderly.

He looked up at me with something like hunger in his eyes. "And...you will be *my* queen, won't you?"

I forced a smile to my lips as I felt my stomach sour. Of course, I had always known it was a possibility that I would marry my brother—and have to fulfill my wifely duties toward him. But now, seeing him this way, as a boy missing his mother, as a child in need of guidance, it was nearly impossible to see him as a man I would have to submit my body to.

"You know I will be," I finally said.

He reached up behind my head and tried to pull me into him for a kiss, but I braced myself and put my finger on his lips.

"Eventually," I said. "But we must wait until we are officially wed." It wasn't true. There were no rules about sex without marriage. I was no virgin. But as far as I knew, my brother was still an innocent, and I was in no rush to educate him about the topic.

He pulled away, disappointed. He went to the mess on the floor and started picking up the papers he had scattered. I walked over and turned the desk upright.

"Lioness of Egypt," he muttered. "What do you think they will call me when I am pharaoh?"

"I don't know," I said. "Maybe you can get into a fight with an animal and name yourself. Maybe fight a jackal and you can call yourself Anubis."

"Or a cobra," he said. "The Cobra of Egypt. I rather like the sound of that."

I laughed. "It does have a nice ring to it."

As we cleaned in silence, I held out hope that everything would work out all right in the end. Father had to make Ramses his heir. It was only right. If Father was determined to not remarry and have another son, he really had no choice in the matter. But no other woman could handle my brother the way I could. I could guide him and direct him and take matters into my own hands behind the scenes if necessary. I would have to eventually overcome my reservations about being his wife and do my duty by my country. My brother might be innocent, but he wasn't stupid. Once we were wed, I would have to give myself to him. At least Father had not set a wedding date yet. After all, Father was still a young man. Still healthy and strong. He would be pharaoh for many more years to come. And my brother was only eighteen. While it was not uncommon for boys and girls to marry at such a young age, my brother was not like other eighteen-year-olds. He needed more time to mature before he could take on the mantle of husband. I would have to speak to Father at some point about how long we could delay the wedding.

But first I would have to find a way out of this war mess. I had almost forgotten that I had promised I would come up with a plan. At least I didn't commit to what kind of plan. He wanted a plan for war. But I would come up with a plan for peace. One that he couldn't reject when I presented it publicly before the ministers. But it would have to be a very good proposal, and I was tired.

When the mess was tidied up, I stood and stretched my back, rubbing my neck.

"I really must retire," I told Ramses. I kissed him on the forehead and then left the room. As I did so, I saw someone rushing down the hallway out of the corner of my eye. I could have sworn it was Keket. Was she looking for me? I started to call out to her, but she was long gone. I shook my head. I was exhausted. Perhaps fighting that lion had taken more out of me than I thought. I would worry about Keket. About Ramses. About Father. About how a lion had gotten into the library in the first place tomorrow.

4

"*H*ave you ever met the tribal kings?" I asked Habibah. We were in my personal study in my quarters of the palace. I had asked her here to help me come up with a plan that would both appease Father and help us avoid war. We were coming up empty.

"Hmm?" she asked, looking up. "I'm sorry. What did you ask?"

"Where were you?" I asked her.

"Just thinking about Psamtic," she said. "It was strange, him not being in the library today."

I nodded. Psamtic was a renowned teacher in the city. He would be given an honorable funeral. I had not met him, but I knew of his work. He and Habibah often had different views of philosophy, but they respected one another.

"I am sorry for your loss," I told her. "I wish I could have done something."

"You did far too much as it was," she said. "Your father never would have forgiven me if anything had happened to you."

"Speaking of Father," I said. "I was asking you if you had ever met the tribal kings."

"Not this generation," she said. "All the old kings died off in the last five years or so. The current kings are all rather young."

"Then how can we possibly come up with a strategy if we don't know them?" I asked, going to the window and looking out at the stars and the moon shining down on the city. It was after dark, but not particularly late. I could see the fires of the marketplace still burning as people continued to shop and eat. Most of the homes lit by oil lamps. "Has Father even met them?"

"Not that I know of," she said. "He has not ventured that far, and the kings have not come here."

"Well, it's simply ridiculous to continue then," I said. "Father should at least send an invitation for the kings to come here for talks before he wages war on complete strangers."

"And will you be the one to tell him how ridiculous he is being?" she asked, raising an eyebrow and doing her best not to smirk.

"Well, I won't use those words exactly," I admitted. "Diplomacy must first be practiced at home before it can be used abroad."

"Wise words," Habibah said. "Wherever did you come up with them?"

"Sometimes I do listen when you speak," I said. There was a knock on the door.

"Enter."

It one of Father's servants opened the door. "The Pharaoh Bakari is asking for you," she said with a bow.

"Now?" I asked, glancing back out the window at the darkening sky.

"Yes, my lady," she said.

I sighed. "Strange. Very well. He must be anxious to know what plan I have devised. Will you come with me, Habibah? He might be less willing to chop off my head if I am accompanied by a renowned wise woman."

"I am not sure I want to be present for this," she said. "But I suppose there should be a witness to your demise."

The servant bowed as we passed and closed the door to my room behind us. When we arrived at Father's quarters, I knocked, but there was no answer. I looked up and down the hall, but I did not see any servants.

"Where is everyone?" I asked no one in particular as only Habibah was around to hear me, and she only shrugged.

I knocked again, but again there was no answer. I cracked open the door. "Father?" I called. The room was dark save a fire in a brazier in the middle of the room. I heard a low breathing, but still, he did not reply.

"Father?" I called again, opening the door a little wider. "Are you ill?"

I stepped into the room, and Habibah was not far behind me. The room was large and open. It was Father's sitting room, where he often came to think or have private discussions. There were two chairs near the brazier and a large rug on the floor. Two bookshelves and a large table made up the rest of the room's furniture. On the far side of the room was a large open window and balcony. Father often came here when he had to contemplate major decisions so he could look out onto the city below and remember the thousands of people who depended on his wisdom. Light from the moon and stars streamed in, and my eyes soon adjusted to the low light as Habibah and I pushed our way further into the room.

"Father!" I said one more time, a bit more forcefully.

What happened next took place in the space of a moment, yet time almost seemed to stand still. In an instant, my whole life changed and there was nothing I could do to stop it. And yet, I saw every single movement. Every step. Every slash of the dagger. As though the entire world was moving through quicksand.

I looked toward Habibah just as Father lunged at her from the shadows, his arm raised high, dagger gripped tight.

"Look out!" I screamed, but it was too late. The dagger plunged into her back before she was even aware of the alarm on my face. Her eyes went wide in shock and her mouth opened in a silent scream. She fell to her knees.

This could not be Father! I launched myself at the man, thrusting my shoulder into him in an attempt to separate him from my teacher. My friend. I took her in my arms as she fell back.

"Habibah!" I cried. I felt my hands grow warm and wet as blood poured from her wound.

She groaned and stuttered. She reached up to my face. "Run..." she whispered.

"No..." I murmured as I started to cry. I could not leave her. I had to find a healer. Someone to save her. But I could already feel her going limp in my arms.

I heard the man who had stabbed Habibah groan. I looked up and saw that he was getting to his feet. I couldn't explain what I was seeing, but it *was* Father. But how could it be? Father would not kill Habibah. I gently laid Habibah on the ground and stood.

"Who are you?" I asked as he took a lumbering step toward me. I stepped back. "Why are you doing this?"

He stepped toward me again, through Habibah's blood

that was pooling around her. He did not flinch or show any sign of remorse. He groaned again, like a hungry dog. As he stepped closer to me, his face was made clear by the light of the brazier. It was Father, but...it wasn't. His eyes were wild, like an animal's. It was as though he was looking at me but could not see me.

"Father," I said gently, and he hesitated in his movements, but only for a moment. "It's me. Sanura. Your daughter. What is wrong? How can I help you?"

He let out a growling shriek and lunged toward me, swinging the dagger violently. I stepped to the side, avoiding his attack, but he twisted and came at me again. I batted his hand away and put my foot in his chest to push him back. He slipped, his feet wet with Habibah's blood.

"Stop this madness!" I ordered, but he only snarled, baring his white teeth at me before lunging at me again. He slashed left and right, wildly, without control. The blade sliced the palm of my left hand. I pulled back and yelped in pain, holding the hand to my chest.

Normally, I would be able to easily defeat a man with a dagger, but I had no weapon, and I had no wish to hurt him —even though he was clearly determined harm to me. I blinked as I suddenly realized that my own father was trying to kill me.

No, this man was not my father. It was his body, but it was not his mind. His wild eyes, his erratic movements, his animal-like countenance. He had finally lost his mind. He had succumbed to the grief and was gone. How had I not noticed just how far into despair he had fallen? As my father, as pharaoh, I thought he was strong enough to survive. But I had been wrong. I had left him to his grief and he had lost himself to it.

He came at me again, striking like a viper. I fell backward onto the floor, the wind knocked out of me, but it also brought me back to my senses. Father or not, I had to defend myself. I had to survive. I had to subdue him so that the priests and healers could help him. Father stood over me and stabbed down with the dagger, but I rolled out of the way and jumped to my feet.

"This is your last warning," I said. "Stop this, or I will be forced to stop you."

Father let out a low menacing laugh. He licked the blade of the dagger, which was smeared with my and Habibah's blood. I grimaced and briefly wondered if there was more at play here. Perhaps some sort of blood magic? I was not versed in sorcery, but many people practiced mysticism on some level. I quickly glanced around to see if anyone else was in the room, but other than Habibah, dead on the floor, there was no one. I saw no talismans or amulets on Father or in the room. I shook my head. It didn't matter. Whatever was causing Father's insanity would have to be sorted out later. He came toward me, and I dropped low, knocking him off his feet. He fell on his back and I was quick to jump up and place my foot on his chest.

"Do you yield?" I asked.

He growled and slashed the knife across the back of my leg. How stupid of me! I fell and he regained his footing. I got up and staggered away, toward the balcony. Again, another mistake! I was now trapped in a much smaller area as he blocked the escape. Forced to fight in close quarters. He came at me again, hacking left and right. If I wanted to survive, I could no longer simply defend myself. I would have to go on the attack. Hurt him. Take him down. I could apologize later. Tell him it was for his own good. As my father, surely he would forgive me.

He came at me again and I grabbed both of his wrists.

He was stronger than I was, and twisted his arms to free himself. But as he did, I kneed him in the stomach which sent him doubled over in pain, dropping his knife.

"I'm sorry!" I yelled, but he did not stay down. He stood back upright and grabbed the sides of my face, headbutting me with his own head. I grunted and stumbled back into the railing of the balcony, my vision going black and my ears ringing. He grabbed my hair and pulled me to my feet. Then my father looked into my face and smiled. He *smiled*. He looked at me with those wild eyes and laughed. My father laughed at the thought of killing me. His daughter. His firstborn. The only child of his first great love. His queen.

I was going to die.

"No!" I grunted. I rammed the palm of my right hand into his nose. His head jerked back and he loosened his grip on my hair. I punched him in the jaw, causing him to release his hold on me completely. I did not continue the attack. I held my hands in front of me. "Enough!" I yelled. But it was not enough for him. He came at me again, his arms wide to grab me. I ducked. He tripped on the dagger he had dropped.

Then he screamed.

He fell over the railing. I stood and reached out to grab him, but it was too late. He was beyond my reach.

"Father!" I screamed as I watched him fall and slam into the ground below. "No!" I cried.

Quickly, a crowd gathered around him. I suddenly realized that people had already been watching us fight on the balcony and they saw my father—their pharaoh—fall to his death. And they were now all looking up at me.

"It's the princess!"

"Sanura!"

"Look! The queen!"

They saw what happened. Did they see him attack me? It was an accident! Self-defense!

"She killed the pharaoh!" someone yelled.

I staggered back out of view of the people below and stepped on the dagger, stumbling. I picked it up and went over to Habibah to see if she was still alive. She could vouch for me that the pharaoh had attacked us, but she was completely limp and already going cold.

"Oh no," I moaned as I held my friend tight to my chest. What had happened? What was I supposed to do now?

The door to the room opened. I looked up and saw Keket standing there.

"Keket!" I said, getting to my feet and stumbling toward her. "Help me! Find the guards. My father...Habibah!"

Keket's eyes were wide as she backed away from me. I looked down and realized I was covered in Habibah's blood and was holding the dagger. I threw the dagger away, but there was nothing I could do about the blood. I followed Keket out into the hallway, still hobbling on my injured leg.

"Wait!" I called to her. "Help!"

"Guards! Guards!" Keket called out. "Sanura has killed the pharaoh and Mistress Habibah!"

"No!" I said, but then I realized that there was no fear, no urgency in her voice. She looked at me with cold dark eyes and I could swear she was smiling.

"What..." I stumbled back. I saw that Keket had a scroll in her hand.

From down the hall, my brother came running toward us. "Sanura!" he called. Then he stopped when he saw the state I was in. "What...what happened?"

"Stay back!" Keket said. "She killed your father!"

"What?" he asked, his face screwed up in confusion.

"No!" I said.

"Yes!" Keket said, grabbing Ramses by the arms and pulling him away from me. "Look at the blood. There's a dagger on the floor of his room. She killed your father. She will kill you! She wants to be pharaoh!"

"I...no...that's not..." I was flailing. Stuttering. My brother wouldn't understand. "He tried to kill me!"

"Father..." Ramses rubbed his head. I could tell he was confused, trying to make sense of it all. I wanted to go to him. Hold him in my arms and tell him everything would be alright. But it would have been a lie. Nothing was ever going to be right again.

The guards finally appeared, and they seemed as confused as Ramses.

"Get her!" Keket ordered. "She killed the pharaoh!"

The guards hesitated.

"Stop!" I said. "It was an accident. The pharaoh, he attacked me and killed Habibah. He—"

"She speaks wicked lies to confuse you!" Keket said. "Capture her before she gets away."

"Why are you doing this?" I asked Keket. I didn't know what was going on, but she was clearly trying to turn my brother and the guards against me. "I...I saved your life."

"You didn't even ask my name!" Keket yelled.

"What?" I asked. What did that have to do with anything? But I didn't have a chance to find out.

Keket stepped forward and read from the scroll, raising one hand high. I didn't understand the words, but I recognized them as Persian. As Keket spoke, her hand began to glow. A strong wind filled the room. There was thunder and lightning. Everyone fell to the ground except Keket, who kept speaking the strange words. Sand filled the room and was whipped up by the wind, encircling me. I looked through the sandstorm and saw my brother cowering at Keket's feet. I reached toward him.

"Ramses!" I called.

"Sanura!" he replied, stretching his hand toward me. But he was too far away.

There was a sudden burst of lightning right in front of me and I screamed. Surely, this was the end. The wind stopped. It was quiet and dark. The only sound I heard was my own breathing. My breathing. I was alive! I opened my eyes and looked around. The only light came from the moon and stars. As far as I could see, there was only sand. I was in the middle of a desert. And I was completely alone.

5

"*R*amses!" I screamed into the night. But there was no one to hear me. There was a little light from the moon and stars, but not much. I shivered and wrapped my arms around myself. I knew that the desert could get cold at night, especially depending on where I had ended up, but this was almost unbearable.

I pinched myself, but I wasn't dreaming. How was this possible? I believed in some forms of magic. I had seen many priests and court magicians perform impossible tricks. Even Habibah—*dear Habibah!*—seemed to possess knowledge beyond that of most people. But to be able to transport someone to another place...that was unimaginable. And that it was Keket who had been able to do so... How? Who was she?

You didn't even ask my name!

A gust of wind picked up and I shrieked, crouching down, afraid the windstorm was going to whisk me away again. But nothing happened. It was just a natural breeze. I raised my head again, but I was shivering. I needed to find shelter. I couldn't do anything in the dark of night. I stood up, my legs a little wobbly. But whether from the shock of what happened or from the magical transport, I wasn't sure. My hand and leg seared in pain as sand invaded the wounds Father had inflicted on me.

I gasped as I caught a glimpse of blood on my hands. I felt the urge to cry and scream, but I stopped myself. I had to focus. Get out of the elements. In the distance, I heard the barking laughter of a hyena. That spurred me to action. I started walking, my feet sinking into the dense sand. I had no idea what direction I was going, or if I would even find shelter, but it was better than sitting exposed, waiting for a hyena to attack me or the sun to rise. It was cold now, but without shelter, the sun would be intense in the morning. I wasn't wearing much since I had just been spending the evening speaking in my rooms with Habibah. I wore a beaded top and a long cotton skirt with a beaded belt. I hadn't been wearing a wig, my own long hair simply plaited. Thankfully I also wore sandals, gold earrings, and gold bracelets and rings. If nothing else, I could trade the gold for food and shelter if I found a village or town. Yes, that is what I would do. I just needed to find somewhere to bed down for the night, something to protect me from the wind and animals, and tomorrow, I would find a more permanent solution. If I just knew where I was, I could then figure out a way home.

The wind whipped up again, and I heard a low growl on the air. I froze. It could be anything. I already knew there were hyenas about, but there could also be jackals. Lions didn't typically live in the desert, but if I was close to the savannah, they could venture into the area looking for prey.

Looking around, I saw some large rocks jutting out of the sand. I gave thanks to Sekhmet, praying that it would provide enough protection to get through the night. I moved around the stones and saw that on the other side, they were jutting out all in one direction, not exactly providing a cave, but an outcropping that would at least shield me from the wind and sun. I moved toward it and stepped inside, sighing in relief. But then I heard a low grinding noise and flew back out of the outcropping just before a saw-scaled viper snapped at my ankle.

I cursed as I reached down and found some small rocks to fling at the creature. It continued rubbing its scales together, making the warning noise once again, and I kept flinging rocks toward it, not bothering to aim since I could barely see in the dark of the outcropping. Finally, the grinding sound stopped. I threw a few more rocks for good measure, but I was finally satisfied that the snake was either dead or had slithered off. I inched my way back into the outcropping and leaned against the side, closing my eyes and taking a few deep breaths.

Finally safe, my head dropped into my hands and I let out a moan of pain. Even if I found my way back to Luxor, my world was crushed. My father was dead! And my brother thought I had killed him! And Habibah! She was dead too, at my father's hand. But why? What happened?

I tried to recall the events of that evening, as painful as they were. Father had mentioned he was tired and had a headache, which was odd. He was never ill, or at least he never spoke of it. But he had been under so much stress, I didn't think much of it at the time and was glad for the opportunity to work with Habibah to try and come up with a plan for the African tribes that might satisfy him. Habibah had arrived and we had retreated to my quarters. I didn't remember saying goodnight to Ramses or seeing Keket. Keket was still learning the ways of the household, so I didn't think it was odd that I hadn't seen much of her. She would most likely be put to cleaning before being trained to wait on me.

When Father sent for me, again, it was strange, but not so odd I felt unsafe. He was the pharaoh and given to flights of fancy and expected to be obeyed no matter the order, no matter the time of day or night. Who was the servant who came to fetch me? I couldn't remember. I wondered if the girl had sensed anything was wrong with the pharaoh. The only way to find out would be for me to get back home and find her to ask.

After I arrived at Father's rooms, he simply attacked us. But...why? I shook my head. I would probably never know now since he was dead. And it was my fault. I hadn't killed him. It was an accident. But I was a better fighter than that. I should have been able to subdue him without causing a fatal injury. General Chike would be so disappointed in me. If I ever saw him again. If I ever had a chance to explain myself.

I shifted on the sand, which felt like it was biting into my skin. I was so thirsty, but had to ignore it. Push through until morning. I just had to hope there was a river or pond nearby.

I remembered Father's eyes. Dark. Wild. Like the eyes of the lion in the library at first. The eyes of a beast. But the lion's eyes had changed. Shifted. Into those of a man. But Father's eyes, they had not changed. Even when I begged him for my life. Even when he stumbled over the edge of the balcony and fell to his death. It was as though he didn't see me at all. Like he was looking through me. As if I were just a piece of meat he needed to devour. I had never been so terrified in my life. So sure I was going to die. What would possess Father to act that way?

Possess? Could he have been possessed by something?

Something evil? If Keket was capable of wielding such powerful magic, who knew what other forces were at work in the palace that night. And what powers might still be in force. What about Ramses? Was he even safe? I had no idea, but getting back to him had to be my top goal. But I could do nothing now. I needed to rest. I needed strength. I would have to find water. A village. A way back home. As soon as the sun rose. I leaned to the side and placed my head on a rock and closed my eyes, willing sleep to come.

 felt as though I had only just fallen asleep when the heat of the day woke me. I wasn't even in direct sunlight, but I was already sweating. I opened my eyes and looked around. I saw the crushed body of the snake and felt a pang of guilt. I prayed to Wadjet, the snake goddess, for forgiveness. I had invaded the snake's home and killed it. It had done no wrong. But I was scared, desperate, and alone. I hoped the goddess would understand.

I stood up and looked around, but saw nothing. Nothing but sand. I walked around the outcropping, my eyes taking a moment to adjust to the bright sunlight. Still, nothing but sand as far as the eye could see. I grabbed ahold of the rock and scurried on top of it, trying to get a better view. Even from on top of the rock, I couldn't see much. But there seemed to be something that looked like grass in one direction. Maybe there was water there, too. With nothing else to go on, I headed in that direction.

I hadn't walked far before I could already feel the skin on my face and shoulders burning. I used my teeth to tear at my skirt, then I ripped part of it free and wrapped it around myself like a shawl. But the material was thin. It wouldn't help much. It didn't take long for me to start licking my lips, desperate for water. But my lips were covered in sand, which only made my thirst worse.

As my eyes focused, I could see some grass waving in the breeze.

"Thank Sekhmet!" I cried as I ran toward it. But as I pushed through the grass, I was met with angry and confused noises from dozens of animals who had also come here to drink. It wasn't a pond or river, just a guelta, a pocket of fresh water that had survived long past the rainy season that could dry up any day. Around the edges of the guelta were foxes, antelopes, and hyraxes. The critters all started when they saw me, but they must have sensed that I was not a threat to them and soon eased back toward the water, though they still kept watchful eyes on me.

I inched toward the water, slowly and without making eye contact with the animals so as not to startle them, and lapped at the precious water like a dog. I had no way to scoop the water other than with my hands, which would only stir up the sandy floor of the pool, and no way to store water for my continued journey. I wondered if I should just stay here and hope that some desert traveler or trader might come my way. But that could be dangerous as well. Who knew what kind of people I might run into. And at night, the predators would come here to drink as well. Hyenas and lions.

The thought of lions made me nervous, and I wondered if my nerves were contagious because I noticed the animals around me growing agitated. I sat up and saw that the foxes had scurried off and the hyraxes were running back and forth along the edge. Several of the antelope had their heads raised, their ears twitching, looking for danger. I listened and looked, but sensed nothing. I was about to return to the water for another drink when there was a sudden splash of water, a scream from the animals, and a guttural growl. A crocodile had lunged out of the small pool and grabbed an antelope next to me and was dragging it into the water.

I screamed and ran from the water, watching in horror as the crocodile rolled the antelope under the water to its death. I put my hand to my mouth and looked around. I now saw the many little eyes and noses peeking up from the top of the water indicating that the pool was infested with crocodiles. *Idiot!* I cursed to myself. I knew that crocodiles could lurk in any water source in the desert, but I had been so thirsty and confused by the whole situation, I had forgotten.

Drenched and thoroughly chastised, I walked away from the pool. The rewrapped wet linen around my head and arms offered some relief from the sun and heat, but it would dry quickly, and I had no idea when—or even if—I would find another—safer—water source. Not to mention food. If I had better survival skills, I supposed I could have eaten that snake I had killed. But I didn't know how to skin it or how to make a fire to cook it over. The guelta was a temporary water source, so even if I dared to go back, it wouldn't have any fish. I shook my head as I started walking in a random direction across the desert.

That night, I slept in a tree. It probably wasn't the safest place. The tree was almost dead, the branches dry. But it was the only way I could have any sort of protection from the hyenas I was sure were following me.

I couldn't see them, but every once in a while, I would hear a yip or a bark coming from somewhere nearby. It was as though they were laughing at me, waiting for me to collapse so they could dig in. Of course, a tree wouldn't protect me from lions or cheetahs, but it was *something*. I had only been lost for a day and was already desperate and losing hope. I was starving. There was nothing to eat. No plants, no animals. And I hadn't come across another water source. And there had been no sign of a village or town. As I tried to sleep, I cried tearlessly. I was too dehydrated to shed tears.

I must have gotten some sleep, though, because when I woke in the morning and descended the tree, there were pawprints around the base of the tree. The wind had distorted them, so I couldn't be sure they were hyena prints, but some large animal had been inspecting me.

I winced as I pulled my cloth around my shoulders, which were red and chafing. My lips were chapped and my legs were windburned. But I had to keep going. I had to find water or a village today. I didn't think I could survive another night in the desert.

I saw waves of heat rising from the sand as I walked. They made me dizzy and a bit nauseous. But that could also be from the dehydration. I nearly laughed for joy when I saw more grass up ahead. I used the last of my energy to run toward it. I would gladly face down a whole bask of crocodiles for a chance at one gulp of water. But as I reached the grass, it faded from view and I realized I was just looking at more sand. It had been a mirage. I nearly collapsed from despair, but then I would surely die. I couldn't stop.

As I walked a little further, I heard a cawing. I looked up and saw a flock of buzzards flying overhead.

"No," I mumbled. Then with more force through gritted teeth, "No! You will not feast on my bones!"

I forced one foot in front of the other. One step closer to water. Or a village. Or a tree. *Anything*. The wind whipped up the sand around me, getting into my eyes and mouth. I sputtered, but had no saliva left to spit it out. The sand blocked the sun, providing some welcome relief, but my eyes burned. My steps grew smaller and I stumbled to my knees. But still, I would not give up. I crawled. One hand in front of the other. The buzzards squawked. I could almost hear Keket's laughter on the wind. I thought about Ramses. I couldn't leave him alone and vulnerable. I didn't know who or what Keket was or what she wanted, but she was dangerous. I had to get back to my brother. I couldn't leave him alone with that...that *sorceress*. And Father. He had died a murderer. A madman. But that wasn't him. Something was wrong with him. Something terrible had happened. I had to go back and clear his name.

And what about my name? People thought I killed my own father! No! I couldn't die with people thinking that of me. I loved my father. My brother. My country. My people. I would die for any of them. They had to know that. I had to survive. Somehow...

I continued to crawl through the blinding sandstorm that was whipping up around me. I was exhausted and felt my arms and legs giving out beneath me.

"No!" I tried to scream, but it came out a whisper from a dry and cracked throat. I strained to look ahead, hoping that if I saw something, it would give me the strength to continue. At first, I saw nothing. But then, something moved. Something dark, like a shadow. It lumbered on four legs. It was big...Like a lion. I gasped, choking on sand. I coughed. When I looked again, the shadow looked like a man, but still walking toward me.

I shook my head and cried. It had to be another mirage. Or worse, a hallucination. I was losing my mind. I laid my head down on the sand and waited for Anubis to claim me.

6

I heard a clacking noise and was afraid to open my eyes. I should be dead. If I were, I had died without the necessary funeral rites or a copy of the *Book of the Dead*. I could never hope to survive the trials that awaited me to see if I was worthy of immortality. I could never accurately recite the seven magic spells that would allow me to pass through Duat, the land of the gods. And forget about having my heart weighed. My last act on earth had been killing Father! Even though it had been an accident, I could feel the heaviness of guilt in my chest. My heart must weigh more than a thousand feathers.

I felt tears run down my cheeks as I began to pant in panic.

"Shh," someone said, gently wiping the tears away. "Shh."

I slowly opened my eyes and was glad to see I was not in hell, surrounded by fire-spitting dragons. There was only an old woman with dark skin and white hair sitting next to me, offering a kind smile.

I tried to speak, but my throat was still raw and parched.

The woman handed me a cup of water, which I tried to drink greedily, but the woman stilled my hand, saying something in a language I could not comprehend.

As I started to drink, I sputtered, choking on the life-saving liquid.

The woman uttered something else and I figured out she was telling me to drink slowly. I sipped the water, even though my body screamed for more. Finally, I fell back on the bed, panting from the effort. I was still so thirsty, but I needed to take the water in carefully lest I vomit it back up. I licked my lips and was surprised that they were clean, not covered in sand. I blinked and looked down. I was covered with a thin blanket, but my bare shoulders were exposed. My beaded top was gone. On my shoulders was a thick green ointment. I touched my cheeks, and the ointment was there as well. It must have been some sort of treatment for sunburn. The hand that Father had slashed with the dagger was wrapped in clean cotton. The woman offered me more water, and I was able to take in more this time, finally starting to feel my thirst quenched. Then, the woman helped me sit up and spoon-fed me some thin broth. It tasted terrible, but I was beyond grateful for the assistance, so I ate every drop.

As I ate and drank, I took in my surroundings. The hut was made of dried mud with small windows cut out for light and airflow, thin colorful curtains hanging over them. There were sticks, shells, and other items dangling from the ceiling like windchimes. They must have been what made the clacking sound that woke me. There were also herbs hung to dry and little birds flitting about. There was a cabinet of vials and apothecary tools. Across the room, there was an altar with candles burning and fruit set as offerings to three large cat-like skulls. Judging by the size of the teeth, I guessed they were lion skulls.

The woman who was helping me must have been a village healer. She wore a red wrap around the front of her head and hair, but the long white tendrils fell down her back. She was older, but I could not tell how old as the woman had no wrinkles in her lovely brown skin.

"Where am I?" I asked, my voice still a whisper. I knew I wouldn't understand the woman's response, but I needed to exercise my voice.

The woman looked surprised that I bothered speaking to her, then she chuckled before responding, talking in a long, winding sentence that I could not hope to understand, but it made me smile anyway.

When I was done eating and drinking—for the moment; I was already salivating for another cup—the woman reached over and patted my cheek and then stood. She handed me a lovely cotton dress with a black and red tribal pattern and some undergarments. She indicated that my sandals were by the door. The woman then left, giving me a bit of privacy to dress myself.

I stood and stretched. I helped myself to another cup of water and then walked over to a full-length mirror to examine my burns. I was surprised that they were not worse. I touched my shoulders and winced, but some of the redness had already faded and the skin was not cracked. The green ointment was working wonders. I would have to find out if I could take some back home with me.

Home.

I sighed at the thought. I still didn't know where I was. I hadn't even considered that I might not be able to communicate with the people I came across.

I touched my cheeks and was glad to see that the redness there was fading as well. I had always taken such pains to keep my skin white. Exfoliating each time I bathed and rubbing my skin with milk. Anat would be so disheartened to see it stained by the sun. Still, I was lucky to be alive at all.

I put on the undergarments and then gently pulled on the dress, careful of the shoulder straps on my burned skin. But, thankfully, the light material didn't put much weight on the burns.

I jumped when I heard someone clap his hands just inside the door flap. I turned and wrapped my arms around myself, feeling exposed in the unfamiliar clothes. I realized that the clap must have been the man's way of knocking without a door frame.

"Yes? You may enter," I said even though I didn't think he would understand. The man entered and my heart stopped in my chest. He was one of the most handsome men I had ever laid eyes on. His complexion was dark, with skin like polished obsidian. He was at least a head taller than me. His hair was cut short and he had a short beard and mustache. His neck was thick and muscular, which led me to believe his chest and arms were muscular as well, even though he was wearing a long red and purple robe.

Purple! Was the man royalty? The tribal leader? What should I do? I had never met another royal outside of the palace before. And would he even understand me? My mouth went dry again as I panicked over what to do.

"My lady," the man said in a smooth baritone as he offered me a polite bow. "I am King Zakai, of the Anwe tribe."

I nearly gasped at his perfect command of my language. His slight accent only made it sound more beautiful to my ears.

"Are you still parched?" he asked as he walked over to the small table by my bed and poured out a cup of water, which he then handed to me. I gulped it down, grateful to have a moment to collect my thoughts.

"Th-th-thank you," I finally said. King Zakai! This was one of the African kings Father wanted to wage war against. What should I do? It seemed rude to say nothing. But would he be angry with me if he knew who I really was? Would he hold me prisoner? For ransom? If Father had been alive, I would be a valuable bargaining chip. But now, would he even know Father was dead yet? How fast did word travel through Africa?

I then gasped, nearly choking on the water as I realized where I was. If I was in Anwe village, I was all the way on the other side of the Sahara Desert, far to the west. Keket had truly impressive powers. I shook my head. Too many thoughts were flooding my mind at once. I needed to take it one step at a time.

"Are you all right?" Zakai asked me as I sputtered.

"Yes," I finally said and offered him a small bow. "Your Majesty. I must thank you for saving me. I thought I was going to die out there."

"You nearly did," he said. "If I hadn't found you when I did..." He shook his head at the thought.

"Well, thank you," I said.

"How did you come to be out there?" he asked.

"It...it's a long story," I said, not wanting to tell him I had been transported by an evil sorceress. Suddenly, even thinking such a thing sounded crazy. "I just want to get home."

"Where is home?" he asked me casually. Almost too casually. I glanced at my pale skin in the mirror and thought about the beaded top and belt I had been wearing.

Surely he had already deduced where I was from. Was he testing me to see if I would lie to him? I then realized that my gold rings and bangles were gone. I was trapped here.

"I'm Egyptian," I said. "And I would like my items returned to me."

He laughed, a loud, clear sound. He then offered me a small key. "They are in the box by your bed."

I looked over and saw that there indeed was a small black lacquered box with a keyhole by my bed that I hadn't noticed before. I took the key and nodded my thanks.

"My mother said that your clothes were beyond salvaging," Zakai said, "but your jewelry we locked away for safekeeping. You may take an inventory if you wish."

"No," I said, placing the key in a little pocket of my dress. "I believe you. I am just...disoriented."

"The desert can do that to you," he said. He then went to the hut flap and opened it. "If you are feeling up to it, would you walk with me?"

I was still thirsty, and hungry, but I didn't want to miss an opportunity to get to know King Zakai better. And hopefully convince him to allow me to return home.

The village was constructed of permanent mudbrick buildings with thatched roofs. A group of children ran up to us and begged of the king with happy smiling faces. He reached into his pocket and handed them some sort of treats, which they all ran off with to eat and fight over. I couldn't help but laugh. It was such a different setting from Luxor. Father rarely interacted with the people so closely, and children would never treat him as a kindly friend. That would be dishonorable! The pharaoh was considered nearly god-like to our people.

The children and women were all dressed in light cotton clothing, similar to what I was now wearing, but they were all in bright colors. The thin fabric was easy to wear in such hot weather. The men dressed in cotton as well, but they wore more muted colors. Everyone smiled and spoke to the king, but they regarded me with a cool indifference. I didn't blame them. They had no idea who I was or if they could trust me. I felt much the same about them. While the king and his mother had been kind enough to save my life, I feared what they might do when they found out who I was.

We walked to the edge of the village and looked out over the vast grassland and tall trees. I knew we were not far from the desert, but the land here seemed so different. I nearly shuddered at the thought of what I had been through over the past two days. The sand. The wind. The snakes. The crocodiles. I dreaded the idea of leaving this safe place again so soon, but I needed to get home. My brother needed me.

"I was hoping you could help me arrange transport back to Egypt," I said. "I can use my jewelry to pay for it."

Zakai nodded but didn't look at me. He was silent for a moment. "From the clothes you were wearing, my mother believes you are a high-born lady," he said. I did not respond, which he took for confirmation and continued. "In that case, you are probably aware of the recent hostilities by Egypt toward us."

I nodded. "I am aware that the pharaoh values your lands," I said. "But I do not support his actions against you."

"I am glad to hear that," he said. "But now that you have been here, have seen our village, our people, you know that it would be dangerous for me to allow you to return. You could expose our secrets to the pharaoh."

"What secrets?" I asked. "That your mother is a healer and you speak Egyptian?"

He scoffed. "You never know what one kingdom could leverage as a weapon against another."

"I am not threat to you, King Zakai," I said. "I only want to go home."

"Then tell me who you are," he said.

I closed my mouth and turned away from him, back to the grassland.

He nodded. "That is what I thought. It is no accident that you ended up here. You are either a spy or were sent here for a much more devious purpose."

"Like what?" I asked, bristling.

"To kill me," he said.

"I didn't even know who you were before you told me your name," I said.

"So you say," Zakai said. "But that is something an assassin would say."

I shook my head and couldn't help but smile. He was teasing me, but he also was not. If he didn't know who I was, he could only assume I was a threat of some sort. Perhaps he wanted to believe I was simply a hapless traveler, but the safety of his people had to come first. I understood and respected that.

"Telling you who I am will not help my case," I finally said. "It could put me in grave danger."

Zakai turned me toward him, holding my forearms gently yet firmly and looked deep into my eyes. "You will always be safe here," he said. "You have my word."

I felt all of my defenses fall. I had never trusted a man so completely. Maybe it was foolish. Dangerous. Stupid. But I was completely alone in the world and needed an ally.

"I am Sanura," I said. "The daughter of Pharaoh Bakari."

Zakai released me a took a step back. He rubbed his chin and looked away. Then he looked back at me, his brow furrowed. If he had not been such a strong man, I thought he might have passed out from the shock.

"Are you lying to me?" he asked.

"Why would I?" I asked. "Would not the pharaoh's daughter be the ultimate bargaining chip?"

"How in the world did you end up here?" he asked. "*Why* are you here?"

"That is a long story," I said. "And I am not sure I believe all of it myself."

"Tell me," he said. "I will believe you."

"The pharaoh is dead," I said.

"What?" he asked, shocked. "How?"

"He...he went mad," I said, tears welling to my eyes. I realized this was the first time I had spoken of Father's death out loud. I clapped my hand to my mouth to stifle the cries. "He attacked me. Killed my teacher. He tried to kill me. We struggled. He fell to his death from the balcony of his room. It...it was an accident! You must believe me."

"Shh," he said, pulling me to him. And I had been right —he did have a muscular chest. "I believe you. Power can corrupt even the strongest of men."

"No," I said, pulling away and looking up at him. "There was something else. Something in his eyes. He wasn't himself. I think...I think he may have been possessed."

He nodded thoughtfully. "A man like that would have many powerful enemies. What happened next?"

"Keket, my slave," I said. "I thought she was just a girl. But now I'm not so sure. I think she may be a powerful sorceress. She blamed me for Father's death. My brother, I think he believed her. I was covered in blood. But then she used magic and transported me to the desert."

Zakai sighed. "That is powerful magic," he said. "Where did you get this slave?"

"She was being beaten by her master in the market-place," I said. "I saved her. She had only been in my household a few days. She is so young. Just a girl."

"Maybe she was using magic to appear young," Zakai said. "If she has the power to transport you across the desert, she could have the power to do anything."

I nodded. "I hadn't thought of that, but you are right. Who knows what she is capable of."

"It could be dangerous for you to go back," Zakai said. And I knew he was being sincere, not merely wanting to keep me captive with him.

"I know," I said. "But my brother, Ramses. He will be the new pharaoh. He could be under her thrall. I had seen her lurking around his quarters. I didn't think anything of it at the time. But I think she may have been trying to turn him against me."

"She killed one pharaoh, banished the queen, and now controls the new pharaoh," Zakai said. "I think we know her motivation now. She wants to control Egypt."

I paced. Zakai was right, but I didn't want to believe it. I had to be missing something.

"I don't know," I finally mumbled. "I don't know. I just need to get home. I need to protect my brother. He's not strong."

Zakai frowned and I realized that he still was not keen on letting me go. I looked back toward the village and realized that it might not even be in his power to release me. Like Father, he would have advisors and ministers to answer to as well. By now, certainly all of them knew I was Egyptian and probably saw me as a threat. He couldn't simply let me return to my country without some reassurance that I would not betray them.

And in truth, I didn't know if I could return home. Keket

had banished me once, she could surely do it again. And next time, I might not survive.

"I don't know what to do," I said. I was confused, scared, and exhausted.

"Come," Zakai said, taking my hand and looping it through his arm. "Eat. Drink. Rest. We will consider our options when you have a clear head. Just know that you are safe here. And you can stay as long as you need."

"Thank you, Your Majesty," I said as we approached the healing hut I had woken up in.

"Call me Zakai," he said as he released my arm and kissed my hand.

"Zakai," I said in almost a whisper, and I thought I saw him tense up as his name rolled off my lips. He then bowed and quickly left. I went back inside the tent and poured myself several cups of water.

7

After I had crawled back onto the bed—which was a reed mat on the ground to protect from the sand and then layers of handmade quilts, both for comfort and for warmth at night—I fell asleep quickly. My mind was in turmoil, but I was exhausted and felt safe here. It was strange. I barely knew Zakai. We'd only had one conversation. I shouldn't trust him so easily. As the daughter of a pharaoh, I had been taught to be more cautious than that. I should know better. After all, I had trusted Keket as well. I never imagined that a slave in need of my assistance would betray me so completely or so quickly. Zakai was probably right. Keket was not what she seemed. I tossed and turned over these thoughts until I fell into a deep sleep.

I slept, but had terrible dreams. Dreams of Father, failing to pass the trials through Duat. Of him passing into immortality but quickly perishing thereafter since he had no food or money to assist him. Of him reaching out for Anat but falling just beyond her reach into a fiery pit below. I didn't believe that Keket would make sure that Father had a proper funeral, and Ramses wouldn't know how to oversee such an event.

Dear Ramses. I dreamed he was being tortured by Keket. Locked away in a small dank cell with no one to care for him. Scared out of his mind.

And I dreamed of Keket herself. A creature of darkness and shadow. A slippery serpent striking at those who had offered her a helping hand. I tried to run away, dodging the serpent's strikes, but I quickly grew exhausted. I had been through so much. I was so tired.

Suddenly, a lion. No, two lions! A third lion! Three lions attacked the shadow snake Keket, ripping at her with their powerful claws. Biting her with their strong jaws. They ripped her into a million pieces. Then, I was safe. The lions formed a protective circle around me, and I was able to sleep.

*W*hen I awoke, I felt rested and hydrated. But I was famished, ready for some real food. I got up, dressed, and stepped out of the hut and into the sun. I didn't think I had slept very late, but the sun was already hot. I raised my face to it and gave thanks to Ra that I was alive to enjoy this moment.

I looked around the village, wondering where I could get something to eat. There was no marketplace. The village was too small for that. But I saw many people tending to their daily work. Women were washing clothes in large tubs outside their dwellings. Men were herding goats in the distance. Children—boys and girls—were sitting on benches in front of a village eldress who was giving them a lecture. I tried to make eye contact with the villagers, and while many smiled back politely, they still did not approach me or speak to me. I wondered if they all knew who I was now. I imagined that in such a small community, it was probably difficult to keep anything a secret for long.

"There she is!" Zakai said, approaching with a bright, shining smile. "I thought you would sleep the day away."

"What time is it?" I asked, looking up at the sun.

"About eight in the morning," he said.

"It is still early!" I exclaimed.

"Here, the sun rises early," Zakai said. "As do we all. But we all take a rest in the afternoon since it grows so hot."

"I will try to wake earlier tomorrow," I said, "so your people will not think I am lazy."

"They do not hold the need for rest against you," he said. "You survived the desert. They respect you for that."

I tried to catch eyes with a woman walking past us, but was unsuccessful. "I'm not sure respect is the word I would use."

Zakai chuckled and motioned for me to follow him. "Give them time. They will warm to you. Come. You must be hungry."

"Oh yes!" I said more eagerly than I meant to and then blushed. "I mean...yes."

Zakai chucked again, and I was sure I'd never be able to get enough of that sound. He led me to another hut and motioned for me to sit on a bench outside while he went inside. He returned with a plate of food, but no utensils. I was starving, but hesitated out of politeness.

"Eat," he said, and I realized that they did not use utensils, but ate with their hands. I was so hungry, though, I didn't mind. I bit into a large cut of unfamiliar meat that was simmered in spices that made my tongue tingle. I moaned with pleasure.

"This is so good," I said, my mouth half full of food. "What is it?"

"Warthog," he said without humor.

I paused for a minute and looked at him. When I realized he wasn't joking, I waited for my stomach to revolt, but it did not, so I continued eating, eliciting another chuckle from Zakai. I realized that I was so hungry, he could have told me it was ostrich butt and I would have eaten it. I wondered if the warthog would taste just as good tomorrow when I was no longer dying of starvation. There was a large piece of flatbread to accompany the food, as well as some fried millet. I ate every bite and even licked the plate, then sucked on my fingers. Zakai handed me a cup of amber beer, and I drank that down as well.

"Do you need more?" Zakai asked me when I was finally finished.

I shook my head, the food making my body feel heavy but the beer making my head float. "No. I just need a moment. It has been so long since I've eaten."

"Take your time," he said, taking the plate from me and putting it back in the dwelling before returning to my side.

"Is this your home?" I asked.

"Yes," he said. "I live here with my mother."

"Your mother?" I asked, surprised.

"It is our way," he said. "We live with our parents until we are married."

I nodded. "I see. I thought I was staying in her home when I arrived."

"No," he said. "That is the healing hut. Anyone in need of care is taken there for quiet and rest. And Mother is our healer, so she does spend a lot of time there. You may call her Tabia."

"Tabia?" I asked. "Is that her name?"

"Sort of," Zakai said. "It is her title as healer. It means 'gifted one.' But she uses it as her name as well."

I nodded. "So, if you still live with your mother..." I hedged, "you are not married?"

He smiled. "I am not. As much as she and the rest of the women wish I were."

"Maybe that is why the other women are looking at me the way they do," I said. "Or...not looking at me, I should say. They probably see any new woman as a potential rival."

"Here, who we marry is our choice," he said. "We never force anyone to do anything they do not wish. When I marry, everyone will know it is because I willed it."

"I also noticed that your girls are educated," I said, motioning to the gathering of children with the eldress across the village. "That is very commendable."

"Why?" he asked, confused. "Women have brains just as we men do. Why should they not be educated?"

I chuckled ruefully. "I would agree with you, but many people would not. I was educated because I was a pharaoh's daughter. Most Egyptian girls are not so lucky."

"Would you like to sit in on the class?" Zakai asked, standing and offering me his hand. "I think the children would find it amusing."

"I wouldn't understand what the teacher is saying," I replied, but I didn't miss the opportunity to put my hand in Zakai's.

"What better way to start learning than by going to school?" he asked. "But I will translate for you until you get the hang of it."

I smiled up at Zakai as we walked back to the makeshift schoolyard. This time, I couldn't help but look up at him, grateful for his kind assistance. I didn't even know if the other villagers were watching us, though I could almost feel their eyes on me. I didn't care. I wasn't one of them, and I wouldn't be staying. Eventually, I would need to go back home to my own people. My brother. The boy I was supposed to...*had* to marry now that Father was gone. My heart hitched a bit in my chest, but I did my best to ignore it, trying to just enjoy this moment of safety and serenity with Zakai. No, the other women did not need to worry that I was a threat. I would be gone soon enough.

We stepped over a low fence around the yard, which probably was only to keep errant goats and chickens out, and took a seat on a rough bench in the very back. The children, all dressed in lovely, colorful dresses and robes, looked at Zakai and me and giggled. I gave some of them a finger wave and they waved back as they whispered to one another about their strange guest. They all had little slate tablets and chalk for writing.

The eldress, who was ancient if she was a day, with skin like tree bark and white curly hair cut nearly to her scalp, clapped her hands and said something to get the children's attention. The children all turned to her and sat up straight as the eldress continued her lesson.

"You will enjoy this," Zakai whispered to me. "She is telling them the legend of the Lion Queen."

"The Lion Queen?" I asked, intrigued, remembering the alter with the lion skulls in Tabia's healing hut.

The eldress moved her hands as she spoke, leaning on a cane. She wore a colorful handwoven blanket draped over her shoulders in spite of the heat. She spoke animatedly, capturing the attention of the children so they soon forgot their guests.

"In the old days," Zakai translated in a low voice, "the gods and goddesses walked among humans, teaching them, helping them, and even loving them."

I felt my cheeks blush.

"At that time, all of Africa was united as one tribe. And the most powerful man of all was the king, who resided in the central plains," Zakai continued.

I laughed as one of the boys jumped from his seat and flexed his muscles in imitation of the great king. The eldress took a playful swipe at the boy and he returned to his seat.

"The queen of all gods knew that trouble was brewing in the land," Zakai went on. "Outside forces were encroaching on Africa, bringing divisions and disharmony. So, to protect the country, the queen of all gods married the king, becoming the Lion Queen. She bore him three sons, the first of the lion kings."

At this, the children all roared and snarled, baring their teeth at each other and holding their fingers like claws, each trying to be the fiercest of the lion kings.

"Hush, hush, hush," the eldress said, and Zakai continued the translation.

"But it was not enough. The lion blood passed from father to son for many generations, but eventually the country fell into chaos, breaking into thousands of tribes. The Lion Queen wept for her people and her children and returned to the mountain of the gods, never to be seen again."

"That is so sad," I said.

"Today, every tribe worships something different. The gorilla. The crocodile. The mighty eagle. But only the few, the true heirs of the Lion Queen, worship the lion."

I chuckled. "So, you are the true heir of the Lion Queen?" I teased.

"I like to think so," he said.

I pressed my lips and thought about this for a moment. "You know, when I was dying in the desert, just before I passed out, I saw a mirage. It was a lion, but then it was a man. That was when I knew I had lost my mind and was going to die."

Zakai put his arm around my shoulders, but gently so as not to hurt my burns. "That must have been terrifying for you."

I nodded. "It was, but probably not for the reasons you think. I was not scared to die. When you are the daughter of the pharaoh, you must always be prepared for death. To sacrifice for your people is the greatest honor. Only a few days ago, I faced a lion that had somehow broken into the city library and I didn't hesitate, knowing it could kill me."

"There was a lion in the library?" Zakai asked, amazed.

"Yes," I said. "I never found out how that happened. Anyway, my point was that I was worried for my brother more than anything. He is alone, in the clutches of that witch. He is a simple man. He cannot rule the empire without me. And what about all the people of Egypt? How will they fare with that madwoman in the palace?"

My eyes started to water, and Zakai held me closer. I buried my face in his chest and let the tears flow. I suddenly realized that I had not had time to mourn Father. Or Habibah. They had died and then I had been banished to the desert and had to fight for survival. Then I found myself in Anwe village and had to be on my guard, learn who I could trust and find out if I was safe.

Finally, I was relaxed and secure in this place. At least for the moment. And I was free to let the tears fall. Zakai wrapped his arms around me and let me cry. He did not try to shush me or offer hollow words of comfort. There was nothing he could say that would lessen my pain. All he could do was give me space to grieve.

I cried out my pain. My fears. My great losses until I

could cry no more. When I pulled away, I saw that the children had gathered around me, and the eldress did not chastise them. I wiped away the tears and the children all moved close, hugging me in small groups. I could not help but laugh at this outpouring of love and support.

"Thank you," I said to each one of them, squeezing their hands and patting their cheeks. Some of the children reached out to touch my pale skin or pet my smooth hair. They pointed out that I was developing little brown spots—freckles—on my cheeks, and I knew that Anat would have been displeased. Still, at least I had survived my time in the desert. Better to have freckles than be dead.

Finally, the eldress clapped her hands and said something to the children. They all dispersed, leaving the schoolyard and heading to their waiting parents or to their huts.

"What is going on?" I asked as Zakai pulled me up to standing as well.

"Midday meal and a rest," he said. "Let me escort you back to your hut."

This time, as we walked through the village, the people who looked back at me had different expressions on their faces. No longer did they look at me with disdain or mistrust, but I saw kindness, sympathy, and even smiles. My outpouring of grief was something that transcended language and culture.

When we arrived at the healing hut, Zakai gave me a polite bow.

"I will have food brought to you," he said, but as he turned to leave, I grabbed his hand.

"I...I'm not hungry," I said. "But I would rather not be alone, if that is alright with you?"

Zakai stepped into the tent and pulled the flap closed

behind us. He stepped up to me and gripped my forearms tightly.

"Are you asking me to stay with you, Queen Sanura?" he asked in a voice that was low and warm.

"Right now, I need nothing more than a lion king," I said.

He lowered his head to my cheek and smelled my skin, my neck, my hair. I could feel his hot breath on my skin, and it warmed my whole body.

"I would not want to take advantage of you in your grief," he said.

I shook my head and placed my hands on his waist. I felt his body stiffen at my touch. "I want it. Want you. Need you," I said. "Comfort me. Keep me safe."

"Love you?" he asked, his lips nearly on mine.

"I wouldn't go that far," I said. "Not yet."

He kissed me, hard and deep, a low guttural growl emanating from his stomach that reverberated through my body. He held me firmly against him, and I felt his rising desire pressing into my stomach. He kissed my cheek, my jaw, my neck. He gently lowered the straps of my dress over my shoulders. The touch of his fingers on my still raw skin caused me to whimper.

"I'll be gentle," he whispered.

"Not too gentle I hope," I whispered back.

He smiled and pulled my dress down, exposing my breasts. My nipples hardened with the exposure to the air, which should have been warm, but felt cool because my blood was on fire. Zakai resumed kissing my neck and chest as he massaged my breasts. I reached up and undid his collar, but my fingers fumbled with the unfamiliar clasps. Zakai obeyed, though, and undid the clasps himself, then pulled the regal robe over his head.

I felt my body go weak at the sight of him. His chest and arms were bulging with muscles, and his stomach was tight and rippled as he moved. The light glistened on each and every inch of his rock-hard body, which was covered with a slight sheen of moisture, causing the deep black skin to take on almost a platinum shine. I ran my hands over his chest and stomach with a light touch. I had never seen a man built quite like he was. Even my own warriors were not nearly as tall, broad, or well-defined.

Zakai then removed my undergarments, fully exposing my naked body to him. I had never been self-conscious about my body. I ate only what I needed and trained with Chike regularly, so I had always considered my body to be desirable. But now, I was completely vulnerable to this mountain of a man. I started to pull my arms up instinctually to cover my chest, but Zakai placed his hands on mine and lowered them. My nakedness should have made me more self-conscious, but the way he looked at me, his pupils large with desire, put me completely at ease. He ran his fingers down my trembling stomach and lightly brushed my black maidenhair.

I couldn't help but moan out loud. I was dying to see his manhood. To touch it. To feel it inside me. I tentatively reached out to his undergarment, licking my lips in anticipation. He stood firm, a cocky smile on his face as though waiting for my reaction. I pushed his garment down and nearly fainted when I saw the size of him.

He was already fully aroused, the blood veins of the shaft running like mountain ranges from the base to the head. The head was smooth like a polished stone. I ran my finger along the shaft and over the tip of the head, and Zakai panted, a drip of juice pearling at his opening.

Zakai then lifted me in his arms and carried me to the

bed on the floor. He lowered me gently onto the bed, then pinned my arms above me. I opened my legs to him, and he positioned himself between them. He skillfully teased my opening, running his manhood along my slit and pearl. He lowered his body onto me, and I delighted in feeling our bare flesh together. I spread myself wider, wanting to feel every inch of him against me. He licked along the length of my neck and then blew on the wetness. My body erupted in gooseflesh. Then he began to enter me, slowly and methodically. He pushed into me and then pulled back. Then he pushed a little deeper, before pulling back again. I was so wet, he could have slid his entire girth into me at once, even as large as it was, but the teasing nature of it caused my muscles to contract, increasing the pleasure.

Finally, he plunged fully into me, and I gasped, my muscles tightening and my back arching. I wrapped my legs and arms around him, matching my body's rhythm to his as he rocked back and forth, thrusting and retreating, over and over again until my whole body was begging for release.

"Yes, yes!" I moaned as I climaxed, grabbing his buttocks and forcing him as deep into me as he could go. He let out a growl like a wild beast as he joined me at the pinnacles of delight.

Together we laid, panting and sated but not wanting to part. Zakai kissed my cheek gently and rose up to look at my face. He ran his fingers through my hair. I pulled his face to mine and kissed him on the lips, my fingers brushing the soft hairs of his chin. He finally rolled to one side, but he continued to hold me in his arms.

"You are amazing," he mumbled into the back of my neck. "My desert flower."

"I can't remember when I was last so happy," I said. And then I remembered all the reasons I had been sad only an hour before. Father. Ramses. Habibah. My near death. Keket. I didn't want to ruin the moment, but a few minutes of pleasure could not erase the troubles in my life. Still, I was safe for now. I snuggled into Zakai's arms for the afternoon rest.

8

I awoke when I heard the sounds of the village waking up. Children were laughing and chattering as they returned to class. Women were washing clothes and pots. And men were calling to the goats as they herded them toward water. I sat up and stretched and took in the sight of Zakai, still lounging lazily by my side with his head propped up under his arms.

"Don't you ever work?" I asked.

He shrugged. "It's good to be the king. I can do whatever I want."

I chuckled and pulled on my dress that had been unceremoniously tossed to the floor. I then walked over to the mirror and found a comb nearby that had been carved out of bone and ran it through my hair. In the mirror, I could see Zakai, in all his nude glory, stand up and stretch, his muscles contracting and relaxing and sending my private place into a spasm again. I looked away and worked on tying up my hair. I found the bottle of green ointment Tabia had used on my burns and reapplied some to my shoulders and face. My burns were much improved, but I didn't want to take any chances with my skin while living in this sunny place. There were few trees and no large buildings to protect me from the sun's rays. If I was outside, my skin was exposed. When I turned back around, I was relieved to see that Zakai had dressed. He was too distracting without his clothes on.

"I hope this isn't going to cause any problems for you," I said. "I know how distrustful people can be of outsiders."

He walked over to me and gently gripped my arms. He kissed my forehead so tenderly, I nearly wanted to cry.

"Do not worry," he said. "The people will grow to love you as I have."

I felt my stomach tighten at the word love. I looked down and pressed my lips together. We had only just met. How could he already be using such a word? Besides, we could not be more than lovers. Eventually, I would have to go back home and marry Ramses. I didn't believe in marrying for love. I would only ever marry for the benefit of my country and people. Even if I didn't marry Ramses, I wasn't sure what benefits a marriage to Zakai would bring. He was a king, yes, but of a small village a desert away from Egypt. I didn't know why Father wanted to make war on such a community; and I couldn't see any reason to align with one so intimately either. The only reason I might even consider marrying Zakai was for love—and that would be foolish.

"Have I upset you?" Zakai asked, concern on his face.

"No," I said, shaking my head and stepping away. "You have been nothing but kind and welcoming. I can never thank you for what you have done for me. But my life, everything, is just so...uncertain right now."

He nodded in understanding. "What is it you want?"

"I want to go home," I said and studied Zakai's face for a

reaction. There wasn't one. "I know you don't want me to leave. Your people might still think I am a danger to them. But even if you did let me leave, I'm not sure how I would go back. The guards and my brother—and by now probably all of Egypt—think I killed my father. I can't just walk in and expect things to fall into place for me. I would be arrested on sight. And then what? I don't know. Is Ramses pharaoh? Is Keket his queen? Is Keket ruling in Ramses's name? Am I overthinking it? Is Keket innocent in all this and truly thought she was protecting my brother from me?" I sighed and paced, my anxiety rising again.

"We need more information," Zakai said. "We need to know the state of affairs in Egypt before you can make any sort of plan."

"Yes!" I said. "Exactly. Thank you. You put into words what I could not express myself."

"I can make no promises of action on your behalf," Zakai said. "I answer to more than just myself. But we can at least start gathering intelligence. But it will take some time. We are a great distance from Egypt. Word does not always travel quickly. And Keket may be keeping many things hidden from the people."

"I am sure she is," I said, but I sighed with some small measure of relief. "But thank you. It is a start."

"Now, come," he said, opening the flap of the hut. "I have work I must attend to. I will take you to Tabia and she can give you something to do to help you pass the time."

Tabia welcomed me into her circle of women for the afternoon while Zakai met with his advisors, ministers, and others. The women showed me how to make a simple straight stitch so I could help sew some children's dresses and robes. I thought it was odd that no one seemed to take notice of the fact that Zakai and I had spent the midday break together. The walls of the huts were thin, and the doors were only flaps of animal skins. Anyone walking by would have known what we were doing. Yet even Zakai's mother seemed not to care a bit. Of course, I couldn't understand what the women were saying about me, even right to my face. They could have been smiling while calling me a shameless whore and I wouldn't know. But I didn't think they were. I found their kindness to be genuine. And I suspected that if anyone dared to insult Tabia's son's lover, she would have had harsh words of her own to impart.

The afternoon passed quickly, and I was surprised when the women began to leave to prepare the evening meal for their families. Tabia took me with her to the hut she shared with Zakai and put me to work chopping vegetables for a stew. By the time Zakai arrived, it was nearly dark, and the stew had simmered to perfection. We three all sat on benches outside of the hut while Tabia ladled us bowls of stew and gave us each a piece of freshly baked flatbread. We talked and laughed together while we ate.

"Mother says that your stitches were quite interesting," Zakai translated for me.

I nodded and took the backhanded compliment as the joke it was meant to be. "I did not had much practice sewing while living in the palace."

"She says that with daily practice, she could have you sewing whole outfits in a week," Zakai said.

"She either thinks better of me than she should or she has a very high opinion of her teaching ability," I replied. Zakai translated for his mother and she laughed.

After we finished eating, I expected them to clean up and toss out any food that might go bad. But I was surprised when Tabia took the kettle of leftover stew and motioned for me to follow her while Zakai stayed behind to clean. Tabia went to the hut of a family with seven children. The father hobbled out on a cane and greeted us. He appeared to have recently broken his leg. Tabia then proceeded to share the extra food with the family. While we were there, another woman visited and brought some sweet cornbread, which the children gobbled up happily. I realized that the village had no people who were homeless or starving. I often saw beggars on the streets of Luxor, but I hardly gave them much thought. While there were some programs sponsored by the temples for the poor and afflicted of the city, some people were just poor, or gamblers, or drank too much, and no amount of handouts could alleviate that. But here, all the villagers cared for each other so that no one was forced to go without. I tried to remember the last time I did anything to help the poor people of Luxor. I remembered that when Anat was alive, she always made sure that money and food were distributed during feast days and holy days. But since Anat's death, I hadn't even considered it. When I got home, I would have to make sure I looked for ways to care for the neediest of my people.

When we were done helping the family, we took the pot back to Tabia's hut to wash, then we went to the village center where a large bonfire was being built. Zakai was there already, visiting with friends. Some young people were practicing a dance and other people were tuning some instruments. As the night grew dark, the whole village seemed to gather at the bonfire for dancing, singing, and music. There were several benches around the fire as well, and some of the women from the afternoon's sewing circle sat with me and tried to teach me some of the words to the songs, but I was a hopeless student and just clapped along as best I could.

While everyone did their best to welcome me and make me feel comfortable, I missed home. I missed reading with Ramses and doing beadwork with Anat. I missed having a steaming milk bath. I missed spending hours in the library with Habibah. I missed overseeing public audiences with Father. I missed looking out my window and seeing the towering pyramids. I missed praying at the southern sanctuary and eating ta'meya and shawarma.

I missed home.

And every moment I was away, my worries over the state of my country and my brother grew. As the music played and I listened to the laughter, I began to feel exceedingly guilty. How could I be here celebrating, having fun, indulging in pleasures of the flesh when my brother could be in mortal peril. I should be doing everything in my power to get home as soon as possible.

I appreciated Zakai saving my life. And in another time, another place, I imagined I could possibly love him. But the cold truth of it was that I was his prisoner here. He spoke of gaining intelligence about Egypt, but if it was safe for me return, would he allow it? I didn't think so. And if it was dangerous to return, would he help me mount an army and fight for my right to return? I doubted it.

Finally, my fears and concerns overwhelmed me and I could no longer enjoy the gathering. I leapt up from the bench and went to the far edge of the village, looking out over the vast grasslands where there was nothing but moon, stars, and silence. Deep in the grass, I caught the twinkling of eyes reflecting the village light. Possibly cheetahs, jackals, or hyenas, stalking the village edge hoping to catch an unsuspecting person foolish enough to wander out of the village at night or trying to steal some unguarded leftovers. A cool breeze brushed over my arms and I tried to rub warmth back into them.

"Sanura?" Zakai said, and I nearly jumped out of my skin.

"You startled me!" I cried.

"Sorry," he said. "But what are you doing out here? Are you not enjoying the evening? Did someone say something to upset you?"

"No," I said, shaking my head. "I was just feeling home-sick. Worrying about my brother...and a million other things."

"I know this is a difficult time for you," Zakai said. "But I am a man of my word. I will find out about the state of your country. I promise. It will just take time."

"I know," I said. "But then what?"

"What do you mean?"

"Will you let me go home?" I challenged. "Give me an army to fight my enemy?"

"Sanura..."

"Am I your prisoner?" I asked, raising my voice.

Zakai gave me a hard look but did not respond. I shook my head and turned away, back to the glowing eyes. But now, I could not see the animals of the night. I was wondering where they went when I felt Zakai's hands on my arms and his chin on my right temple.

"I know you are scared," he whispered, and I felt myself melt into him. I knew I needed to stay strong. Keep him at a distance. He was not my enemy, but he was not yet my ally either. But I could not resist him. "Give me time, Sanura," he continued, my name falling out of his mouth like honey. "We will find a way through this."

I turned to him and looked deep into his eyes. "Zakai..." I started, but I wasn't exactly sure what I wanted to say. I searched for the words, but my thoughts were interrupted by a trumpeting sound.

At first, I wondered if it was an animal bellowing. A rhinoceros or an elephant? But as it grew louder, I knew what it was, and Zakai did too. His grip on my arms tensed and his jaw tightened.

"That's an Egyptian warhorn," I said.

"I know," he said, then he looked at me.

"You can't think..." I started to say. "I didn't lead them here!"

"Then how could they possibly be here?" he asked.

"I don't know," I said. "When Father was alive, the reason he didn't send his army to attack your village was because the desert was insurmountable."

"So how could they be here now?" he asked.

I thought for a moment, but I could only come up with one explanation. "Keket," I said. "If she could transport me here, she must have found a way to transport the army as well."

"One woman cannot possibly transport an entire army across the desert," Zakai said.

"I don't pretend to understand her powers," I said. "I only found out she was magical yesterday!"

"We cannot argue about this now," Zakai said, grabbing my hand and leading me back into the village. As we ran, I could feel the rumbling under my feet of the army approaching.

"Arm yourselves!" Zakai announced as we reached the bonfire. The festive voices and music immediately silenced. "We are under attack!"

The villagers sprang into action. I was amazed to see

that no one appeared to be panicking, but everyone knew their role.

"The women who cannot fight, along with the infirm and the children, know where to hide," Zakai said to me. "Follow Mother."

"I can fight," I said. "I train with Egypt's top general."

"Then come with me," he said, leading me to a hut that served as an armory. A man was already there, handing out weapons to any man or woman who asked for one, along with shields and leather armor. I accepted a shield and a medium-length sword since I did not see a khopesh among the weapons. It was heavy and not what I was used to, but I would get the hang of it.

Zakai barked orders to his warriors in their own language and then ran toward the village border. I had not understood him, but I knew that in battle, there was no time for translation. I simply followed his lead.

We had barely gotten into formation when a volley of arrows fell toward us. Zakai yelled something and raised his shield. I followed suit, guarding myself just as the arrows pierced my shield. I heard screams of pain as some of the villagers fell. My heart burned for those who were being injured or killed by my own men, but I knew I could not be emotional in the moment. I needed to help fight the army back, then we would care for the wounded together.

Yells rang out as the Egyptians stormed the village. Zakai and the villagers let out their own war cries as they fought back. I quickly lost sight of Zakai and focused on fighting one enemy at the time. I used the shield to block a blow and then stabbed. I heard a groan as the sword met its target, then I stepped forward, blocking and striking, blocking and striking. I thought I was making good progress, but when I took a moment to survey the scene around me, I saw that I had fallen back into the village, and the other village defenders had as well, and many were dead. Far more villagers had fallen than Egyptians. They were losing the battle. I looked around for Zakai, wondering if he was giving orders to regroup and refocus the attack. I saw him not far from me, surrounded by dead Egyptians and half a dozen more fighting him at once. I ran toward him to help, but then what I saw made me freeze in my tracks.

Zakai let out a monstrous roar, one strong enough to make the Egyptians stop fighting and put their hands to their ears, then he transformed into a huge lion! I shook my head, unable to believe what I was seeing. If I hadn't lost my mind in the desert, I certainly must be crazy now. But as the lion...Zakai, who was larger than any natural lion, ripped through the bodies of the Egyptians, leaving blood, body parts, and entrails in his wake, I knew that what I was seeing was real. I remembered being in the desert, in the sandstorm. I saw a lion coming toward me. But then I saw a man. I thought it was a mirage. But now I realized it was Zakai.

The lion leapt forward, ripping apart one Egyptian after another. I was suddenly terrified and felt the urge to flee. I knew nothing about this man or his people. Were they all lions? I didn't know, and I didn't care. I just had to run. I had to go home. To Egypt. Oh gods! I had just killed my own people! How could I? I had been so blinded by my affection for Zakai, I was willing to fight and kill my own men! This was why I could never fall in love! Love makes you do stupid, dangerous, foolish things!

I ran away from the village, into the grassland. Into the dark. Among the soldiers and the wild animals. At least I had a sword. I could defend myself if need be. I then felt someone grab me by the shoulders and push me to the ground.

"I have her!" the soldier above me yelled. "I have Sanura!"

I tried to wriggle free, but another soldier grabbed one of my arms, and then another soldier grabbed my other one and they dragged me to my feet. I grunted and fought, but the group of them were too strong for me.

"Take her to the cage and chain her!" another soldier said. "Keket will be pleased."

"Keket?" I cried. "Why are you taking orders from her? I am the pharaoh's daughter! I am your queen!"

"You killed the pharaoh!" someone yelled, spitting in my face. "You'll pay for your crimes!"

"But...Ramses...Keket!" I screamed. "What is going on?"

"Shut it," someone ordered, slapping me so hard my neck made a snapping sound.

"Zakai!" I cried, but I was running out of strength. I was scared and confused. The men dragged me well away from the village and tossed me into an iron cage pulled by two strong horses. They locked and secured the door behind me.

I jumped up and shook the bars, but they held fast. The men laughed at me.

"We will be well rewarded when we return," someone said. Then they slapped the horses and the cage lurched forward.

"Help me!" I yelled as I continued shaking the bars of the cage. "Zakai!"

9

I gagged on the dust from the sand the horses kicked up as they dragged the wheeled cage across the desert, the soldiers running alongside us. It didn't take long for me to realize there was something unnatural about them. They were wearing full armor and had just endured a great battle after traveling all the way to Anwe village from Egypt, yet they were able to run fast enough to keep up with horses? We were also traveling much faster than humanly possible, the errant trees and rocks passing us by at an incredible rate.

I pulled myself up onto my knees and held the bars of the cage tightly. The top of the cage was too low for me to fully stand.

"Hey!" I called out to one of the soldiers. "You know who I am! I am Queen Sanura. And I demand you release me at once."

"We don't take orders from murderers," the soldier replied.

"Then who do you take orders from?" I asked.

"The order to capture you came from the Lady Keket," he said.

"The *Lady* Keket?" I scoffed. "She's nothing but an impudent slave. Why would you listen to her?"

"She is all powerful," the man said, his voice flat and emotionless. "And will lead us into a new age of prosperity."

"Is that what you think?" I asked. "Or what she has ordered you to think?"

The man shook his head and blinked, as though waking from a trance. "What?" he asked.

I only nodded. These men were not in control of their own thoughts or actions. At least not fully.

"You said the order to capture me came from Keket," I said. "What other orders are you following?"

"Pharaoh Ramses ordered us to ransack the village," the soldier said.

So, Ramses *was* now pharaoh. And he was fulfilling our father's dream of overrunning the African tribes. I sank down and sighed. This was a disaster. Keket must be controlling Ramses as well, making him give such a foolish order.

My brother needed me. I did need to return. But if I returned in chains, would I even have a chance to see him? Did he know Keket had ordered my capture? And the soldier called me a murderer. The whole country might believe I killed Father. Keket could order my death as soon as I arrived back in the city without ever giving me a chance to defend myself. Or she could lock me in a dungeon under the palace, have me tortured, and let me die a slow and painful death. Ramses might never know what happened to me.

I had to go back. That much was certain. I had to get to Ramses. But I could not go back as Keket's prisoner. I needed to somehow gain control of the situation. I had to escape. Get help—

A great roar echoed over the sand. The horses whinnied in terror and the men raised their swords in fear.

"Protect the cage!" one of the soldiers ordered. "We must return the prisoner to Lady Keket!"

The horses were pulled to a stop and the men, about a dozen of them, surrounded the cage, assuming a fighting stance.

My heart beat hard in my chest. Zakai! Did I really see what I thought I saw? I hardly had time to think about it. He had transformed into a lion right in front of me and ripped those men limb from limb! How was it possible? Some sort of magic—sorcery!—had to be at work here as well. I needed to get away from here. How could I trust anyone?

The lion roared again and it seemed to bounce off the surrounding sand dunes. The men looked left and right, unable to discern where exactly the roars were coming from. The sun was rising over the desert, setting the sand ablaze in reds and oranges. A shadow fell over us as the giant lion crested a dune and stared down at us.

His mane fluttered in the morning breeze. The rising sun made his tan coat shine like a topaz jewel. Even from a distance, his massive form dwarfed us. A rumbling from deep in his belly reverberated all the way through my bones. He was the most majestic thing I had ever seen.

As Zakai stepped forward, several of the men dropped their swords and ran away. They must still have had some of Keket's power because they were merely a blur in only moments. Two of the men used their swords to cut the horses loose, causing my cage to tip back and slamming me against the bars. The men mounted the horses and rode away.

"Stand your ground, men!" one of the soldiers ordered. Some of the soldiers tried to obey, but I could see their hands shaking and sweat beading on their foreheads. Even though Keket was trying to control them, they had enough sense to know they could not defeat a lion king.

"You should run!" I said to the few men who were remaining. The slight encouragement was all it took to send everyone except the commanding officer heading in the opposite direction from Zakai. Zakai lunged forward toward us, me in the cage and the commander standing nearby.

"Let me out!" I ordered the commander. "Take me with you!"

The commander kept his eyes on Zakai but reached to his belt. "I...I don't have the key," he said. "One of my men had it."

"Then run, you fool!" I said. "He's going to tear you apart!"

"Better than what the Lady Keket will do to me if I return without you," he said.

"Then why are you listening to her?" I asked. "She's a sorceress! A usurper! She's dangerous."

"I...I don't know..." the man stuttered. He stepped back as Zakai approached.

Then, the soldier's eyes went black. He raised his sword and ran at Zakai. Zakai roared and with one swipe, the soldier's chest was ripped open. The soldier collapsed and bled out onto the sand. My eyes lingered on the blood for a moment as it pooled black around him. The sandy breeze continued to whip around my dress, my hair, my fair skin. Like a faint song, I was sure I heard Keket's laugh. I think Zakai heard it too, for when I looked up at him, he was sniffing the air, as though searching for something. Our eyes met, and I fell back in the cage, as far away from him as I could get.

"Stay back!" I ordered.

Zakai chuckled, then he spoke, his lion mouth moving like a human's. "Are you afraid of me now?" he asked.

"How...how is it possible you speak?" I asked.

"How do I turn into a lion at all?" he replied. "I do not pretend to understand the ways of the goddess."

"The goddess," I repeated. "So that story the eldress told the children. It was not merely a myth, but was a—"

"A legend that explains the birth of the lion kings," Zakai completed for me.

"So how do you—" I started to ask, but Zakai interrupted me.

"Do you want to keep talking from inside that cage?" he asked, an annoyed growl to his voice. "Or would you like to get out of there?"

I shrank back a bit. "I think I feel safer in here."

Zakai snorted and then turned his back on me. "If that is how you feel."

"Wait," I said, gripping the bars of the cage at the mere thought of actually being left alone. "No. Of course I want out of here. There is no key, though. The man who had it ran off."

"I make my own keys," Zakai said. He walked up to the cage door and placed his massive paw on the lock. He ripped the lock from the door with minimal effort and the door swung open. Zakai then backed up and let me climb out on my own.

"Thank you," I mumbled as I rubbed my arms. I looked around us. There was nothing but sand in every direction.

"Where will you go now?" Zakai asked.

I looked at him, my mouth agape. I had expected him to force me to go back with him.

"You...you're letting me go?" I asked.

"I will not force you to return with me," Zakai said. "I think you will bring great trouble to my people. But, if you do come back with me, I will do my best to help you."

I looked away from him, back across the desert. My heart yearned to return to Egypt. I could feel it in my bones. In my very soul. Everything in me called me to return home. To Ramses.

But I knew I could not go home alone. I did not know the extent of Keket's powers, but what I had seen already terrified me. I could not return until I knew what I was facing. And I could not stay here in the desert. I would be dead in a matter of days, as I had already learned. While I appreciated Zakai giving me the option of leaving, he and I both knew I had no real choice but to return to Anwe village with him.

I turned my back on Egypt and walked alongside Zakai in his massive lion form. His head was as high as mine. Each step he took left me behind. His tail swished back and forth like a giant fan.

"It will take us forever to get back walking this way," Zakai grumbled.

"What?" I asked. "The soldiers had not been marching for long."

"Perhaps you did not notice from your place in the cage," Zakai said as we crested a dune and looked off at the endless sea of tan sand around us, "but they were traveling at a preternaturally fast pace."

So much had happened to me in the last couple of days, it was starting to all blend together. But I did remember at one point thinking that we flew by some dead trees far more quickly than normal.

"I remember something to that effect," I said.

Zakai started down the side of the dune, his paws spread wide and staying mostly on top of the sand, making it easy for him to traverse the desert. When I tried to follow him, my small feet sunk into the sand, making each step slow and exhausting.

"The sorceress must have been using her powers to make them travel beyond what humans should be capable of," Zakai surmised. "If you try to walk back, you will die."

"What is the alternative?" I asked, already panting despite my best efforts.

Zakai looked at me and then nodded toward his back. "Get on."

"What?" I asked. "You want me to...ride you?"

"You had no problem riding me in your hut earlier," he said and licked his lips.

I groaned. "I *do not* want to think about that right now with you in this...state."

Zakai chuckled. "I am only teasing you. But seriously, come on. You can hold onto my mane. I also have advanced speed. We will be home by sundown." He then laid down, as it would have been impossible to mount him while he stood, as tall as he was.

I hesitated. I could not believe I was about to ride a lion like a horse—a lion that was actually a man. But finally, I took a deep breath and climbed upon him. As he stood, I nearly fell off as I tried to find my balance, but I gripped his mane with my hands and squeezed his sides with my thighs.

"Are you ready?" he asked.

"Mmhmm," I said, not at all sure that I was. Then, he

took off. He was not running. It was more like a steady trot. But we were already moving far more quickly than should have been possible.

"So," I said after a few minutes. "Have you always been a lion king?"

Zakai laughed. "No," he said. "To become a lion king is hereditary, yes, but the power is not active until one is actually a king. I did not have the power to transform until my father died. But I always knew I would be a lion king someday."

"But how?" I prodded. "I know there must be an element of magic to it, but how did your people know about this? How long has it been happening?"

"We have no legends or stories from before the time of the lion kings," Zakai said. "It has always been so. But the power used to be stronger. There was a time when all of the children of the king could transform from the time they could walk—sons and daughters."

"What happened?" I asked.

"There was a great rift between brothers," Zakai said. "Hundreds of years ago. We do not know why exactly they fought, but it led to the formation of the three lion tribes."

"Three?" I asked. "There are two more lion kings?"

"There are," he said. "Currently, one is King Oringo of the Dakari people. They live in the jungle mountains. The other is King Saleem of the Nuru people in the western desert."

"Are you on peaceful terms with them now?" I asked.

Zakai chuckled ruefully. "Not at all. We avoid speaking to each other at all costs."

"Why?" I asked. "You have so much in common."

"Are you at peace with the other humans?" Zakai asked.

"Some," I said.

"And others you fight with viciously," he said. "Just because we share this one similarity does not mean we have enough in common to be allies."

"You have another similarity," I said. "My father wanted to subjugate all of you."

"This is very true," Zakai said. "But thankfully your father is no longer a threat."

"But my brother," I said, "with Keket by his side could be an even more formidable enemy. Look at what's just happened. My father was not able to see his plan through because he could not move an army across the desert. Keket seems to have found a way."

I could feel Zakai growl from deep in his stomach as the vibrations shook my body.

"Keket is a danger, to be sure," Zakai said angrily. "But that does not mean I need the aid of Oringo or Saleem. You and I, Queen of Egypt, we will find a way through this."

I felt my face blush when he called me Queen of Egypt. I looked back over my shoulder toward my homeland. My heart ached for it. I was thankful that I had Zakai by my side, but I needed to return home.

I leaned forward, placing my head beside one of his giant ears. "What's it like?" I asked. "To transform into a lion?"

I felt a shiver run through Zakai's body. "It is like being freed from a cage."

I sat back and thought about the cage he just helped me escape from and could somewhat relate.

"Even when there is no threat," Zakai went on, "sometimes I simply must transform. I feel like I am going to burst out of my skin if I don't. I must take on this form and run and roar and fight and eat or else I will lose my mind."

The thought of Zakai killing and eating a gazelle—or a

man like that soldier—suddenly filled me with dread. He must have sensed my unease because he went on.

"I am fully human," he said. "A civilized man. But I am also a beast. I have to balance my two natures. I cannot be one without the other."

"When I was a child," I said, "my step-mother, Anat, would pray to Hathor. As the wife of the pharaoh, it was only fitting. Hathor was the wife of Ra and considered the queen of the gods. But I always identified more with Sekhmet, the lion goddess."

"Tell me about her," Zakai said.

"Sekhmet is the goddess of war," I said. "Because lions are the fiercest of creatures. Every year, we have a festival in her honor where everyone drinks red wine and the pharaoh pours wine out in the streets and into the Nile River. Sekhmet will drink the wine, thinking it is blood, and she will bring us peace for the coming year."

"Why would you identify with a goddess of war and blood?" Zakai asked.

I laughed. "That is not why I honor her," I said. "But I admire her strength. Her independence. She is also the protector of the pharaoh, like how I wish to protect my brother. Anat worried that my affinity to Sekhmet would irritate my father. But he praised me for my devotion to her. I wonder now..." My mind started to trail off as I thought about Father and Ramses.

"Wonder what?" Zakai asked.

"I wonder if that is why Father made me queen instead of heir," I said. "Instead of pharaoh."

"Can a woman be pharaoh?" Zakai asked.

"It has happened," I said. "But never when a male heir was an option. I had just hoped that, given Ramses's condition, that Father might consider making me pharaoh instead."

"Do you think he made the right choice?" Zakai asked.

"I love my brother," I said. "And I will do whatever it takes to keep him safe from that sorceress."

I realized that I didn't answer his question, but thankfully, he did not press me on it.

"As soon as we get back," Zakai said. "I will talk with my advisors and see what aid we can offer you."

"Thank you," I said. As much as I appreciated Zakai and all of the Anwe people, my only goal was to go home.

10

*M*y relief at returning to the village was short lived. We arrived to the sounds of people crying, and I was forced to remember that it was because of me that my men had brought death to this place. They were not under my orders, but they had been sent here to bring me back to Keket, even though it was she who had banished me in the first place. Perhaps she had meant to banish me even further away. Or had not tried to banish me at all, but do something far worse. Whatever she had planned, something must have gone wrong. She must not have had full control over her powers when she banished me. But who knew how much strength she had gained in the days I had been gone.

Zakai shifted back into a man before we entered the village.

"Are you ready?" he asked me, holding my hand gently.

I had to shake my head to remind myself that everything I was seeing was real. It was almost strange hearing his voice come from his human form after spending the whole day talking to a lion.

"I suppose," I said, shrugging my shoulders. I had no choice but to return to Anwe village. I had nowhere else to go. But would the people accept me now, after what had happened? I doubted it. And judging by the fact that Zakai was holding my hand, I rather thought he doubted it as well and felt the need to demonstrate to the people that I was to be welcomed back.

The bodies of the soldiers had already been dragged out to the desert and buried unceremoniously in the sand. I was glad that I did not have to see them, but my heart ached for them and their families, just as it did for the villagers who had died. If I ever regained my place in Egypt, I would find out who those men were and make sure their families were taken care of.

We passed a hut, outside of which Tabia was washing the body of a dead man. His wife and child were crying by his side. Several women were trying to comfort the grieving widow, but she was having none of it. I was so distracted by the scene, I did not realize that an older woman had approached Zakai and me until she started yelling at him. I turned to her in surprise just as she spat in my face.

I stared at her wide-eyed and wiped the spit away, stepping behind Zakai. Zakai reprimanded her gently, rubbing her shoulders. The woman continued to rant and rave. I didn't know exactly what she was saying, but her meaning was clear. She blamed me for the death of her kin.

The woman hurled a few more of what I assumed were obscenities before Zakai convinced her to return to her home. Zakai then ushered me back to the healing hut. We passed several more families preparing their dead for burial on the way.

"You should stay here," Zakai said. "You will be safe. I

will tell the people that you are in need of protection. They will not disobey me."

"They have every right to be upset," I said.

Zakai nodded. "A mass funeral for the fallen will be held tonight. It might be best if you stay out of sight."

I shook my head. "This is all my fault, or at least this happened because of me. If I cannot take responsibility and look at the faces of those who died on my behalf, how will your people ever trust me again?"

Zakai hesitated, considering the pros and cons of me attending the funeral. "I will speak to my advisors and the families of the dead to see what they think. If they want you to attend, I will let you know. Until then, stay here."

I nodded. I had no desire to cause the people more distress. I held onto his hand for as long as possible. As he left the hut, he looked back at me as though he wanted to say something else, but then he turned and left. I felt a strange desire to say something to him as well, though I did not know what. I just knew that being separated from him caused my heart to freeze. Part of it was fear. I knew that he said his people would not harm me as long as I was under his protection, but was I was not so sure about that. The death of a loved one could cause the most rational person to do unthinkable acts. But also, I missed him. He was an incredible man. Powerful. Handsome. A strong leader. Kind.

And a lion shifter.

I nearly snorted a laugh. How could shifters exist and no one outside the villages knows? Such power. Such magic. It was a gift from the gods. According to the legend the eldress told the school children, the first lion kings were descendants of the Lion Queen, the queen of all gods. Zakai was a child of a goddess. It explained why he was a near perfect specimen of a man. I wondered if that goddess was Sekhmet. But if it was, why would she bless the Anwe people and not the Egyptians? I sighed. Who was I to question, or even try to understand, the ways of the Divine?

I sat on the bed to relax and try to calm my racing heart. But as I ran my fingers over the pillows and blankets, I couldn't help but remember that this was where Zakai and I had so recently made love. My heart started to race even faster as I thought about his hard body and soft lips. I stood quickly, shaking my head. I couldn't think about that now. Maybe not ever again. He was part lion! And the king of a tribe. What we did was enjoyable. Pleasurable. But nothing more than pure lust. Eventually, I would have to return to Egypt. To Ramses.

Oh, Ramses. I began to pace the room. My dear brother. What is happening? Are you safe? The soldiers had said they were following Ramses's orders in attacking the village. That was a good sign...in a way. At least Ramses wasn't locked in some dungeon...or worse. Although Keket was probably using him to achieve her own ends. Hopefully they were not yet married. I wondered if it really was possible for Zakai to learn what was happening in Egypt. Egypt was the most powerful empire in the world. Everyone should know what was happening there. Somehow, I needed to get back to Egypt. Back to Ramses. I had to defeat Keket and resume my place as queen. But how?

I walked over to the altar with the three lion skulls. When I first arrived, I thought the altar was unique. But now, it held new meaning. I reached out and laid a finger on each skull's forehead.

"One...two...three. Three lion kings. Zakai. Oringo. Saleem."

If I was ever to return to Egypt, I could not do it alone. I would need help. After the attack on Zakai's village, I did not think his people would help me. But what about Oringo and Saleem? The other lion kings and leaders of the African tribes Father had wanted to subdue. Of course, I had no idea why they would want to help me either. Why would anyone want to go against the might of the Egyptians?

I felt the stress building in my neck and shoulders. I rubbed them and sighed. It was growing dark, but I could smell the smoke from the many fires burning around the village. I could still hear the wails of those in mourning. They seemed to be growing louder and my anxiety grew. Was I going to be left alone here? Or were they going to come for me? What if Zakai could not convince the people to leave me alone? What if they wanted revenge?

I nearly screamed with fright when Zakai opened the flap to the hut and entered, I had worked myself up into such a frenzy.

"Forgive me," he said, offering me a black dress. "I did not mean to startle you. The people have agreed that you may attend the funeral. They want you to see what your people have done."

"They might mean it as a punishment for me," I said, accepting the dress, "but I will accept it as my penance. I am sorry for the troubles I have brought to you and your people."

Zakai turned his back to me so I could change. I slipped off the colorful dress and quickly replaced it with the simple black frock.

"None of this was your fault," he said. "Keket attacked you and banished you here. You had no control over the matter."

"But Keket is not here," I said as I quickly plaited my

hair and tied it up. "Until she is brought to justice, I am the only person your people can hold accountable for the deaths of their loved ones. I accept that."

Zakai turned to face me and gripped my forearms. He exhaled and placed his forehead against my own. "You are a magnificent woman, Sanura," he said. "And I have not forgotten my promise to help you. But I need time."

I nodded and placed my hands on his waist. "Let us bury your dead first."

He kissed my forehead and led me out of the hut, holding my hand. "Just follow my lead," he said, and I nodded.

The funeral procession was already passing the hut, with many people beating drums. A shaman was leading the way. He was a very old man and had long hair, as though it had never been cut, braided and wrapped around his head. His lips were painted black, but his body was painted in ornate tribal symbols. He wore a long black robe that dragged on the ground behind him and necklaces and bracelets of bone. He was chanting in their tribal language, alternating between raising his hands to the sky and waving them over the earth.

Behind him, the dead were carried on long stretchers by four bearers. They were draped with the skins of animals. Zebras. Cheetahs. Impalas. Hyenas. Alongside each dead person, the family walked. Zakai and I fell into the procession behind the third dead body. I wondered how many more were behind us.

"We bury our dead as quickly as possible," Zakai explained, "so they don't turn into angry ghosts and can make their way to the afterlife. They must be buried properly, or they won't be able to journey to the land of the dead."

"We have similar beliefs," I said. "The journey to the afterlife is very difficult and must be done exactly right." Not for the first time, I marveled at how similar our beliefs were.

Even though it was a very dark night, there was no problem having enough light to see by. Large braziers and bonfires were lit throughout the village and along the procession site to the cemetery, and many people also held torches or candles. Still, as we left the village, I could not help but feel apprehensive about what could be watching us beyond the light in the darkness. I looked out into the tall grass and saw glowing eyes looking back at me. I squeezed Zakai's hand tightly, and I felt him squeeze my hand back, but he kept his eyes straight ahead. I seemed to be the only person worried about what lurked in the dark. But I soon realized that we were very great in number. The entire village was taking part in the procession. We had plenty of light from all of the torches, and we were making a great noise with the lamentations of the grieving families and the banging from the drums. No animal would be foolish enough to attack.

When we arrived at the cemetery, a dozen graves had already been dug. The dead were lowered into the pits, and their family members kneeled beside them. The hair of every family member was then cut and thrown into the graves. Everyone then helped fill in the graves. Nearby, a large fire was started, and I saw that clothes, furniture, food, and other household goods were being tossed into it.

"Everything the dead will need in the afterlife," Zakai explained. I nodded since we also buried our dead with their possessions, but we did not burn them. Everyone then made their way back to the village. Along the way, I had to be careful where we stepped as people dropped items in the path, such as branches and brambles.

"Those are to keep the dead from returning to the village," he said. "To encourage them to journey to the next life."

As we entered the village, the shaman washed everyone's hands, feet, and faces with water steeped with aloe to cleanse us of the funerary dust so we would not bring bad luck back to the village. A large feast was then held to honor the dead and their family members. I ate very little. Even though I was starving—I had not eaten since before I had been taken by the soldiers—it felt wrong for me to partake of the food meant to honor the dead who had died because of me.

I excused myself as soon as it was not insulting to do so and went back to my hut. I collapsed onto the bed and cried. I was exhausted. I was overwhelmed. I was scared. The burial had reminded me that I did not take part in the funeral for Father or Habibah, if they had funerals at all. What would happen to them if they were not given the proper funerary rites? Would they linger in this world forever? Would they haunt me? Would they be tortured by the demons of Hell? I didn't want to think about it, but I couldn't stop. There could still be time to make sure they were given the proper funerary rites. It would take the priests months to mummify the bodies. If I could get back to Egypt, I could make sure they were buried and honored properly. But *how* could I ever get back? And who knew? Maybe Keket and Ramses made sure that Father and Habibah *were* being honored in death. But I had no way of knowing, and I would not be there. I would not get to say goodbye to them.

My back was to the door of the hut, but I still heard Zakai enter.

"Sanura?" he called out.

I wiped the tears from my face but I did not face him. "Yes?" I asked.

"Are you all right?" he asked.

I chuckled ruefully. "No," I said. "How could I be?"

"The people's anger will cool in time—" he started to say, but I cut him off.

"It's not that," I said, sitting up and facing him. "Not *just* that anyway. It's everything. My life has been utterly destroyed and I see no way back. I can't even see any small steps I can take toward putting things right. I need to return to Egypt. But how? And if I did, what would I do then? I am trapped here. I might not be a literal prisoner, but I have nowhere to go and there is nothing I can do. I have never felt so helpless."

Zakai sat next to me and put his arm around me. I couldn't help but sigh in contentment. The warmth and weight of his arm instantly put my mind and body at ease.

"I do have any idea that may work," he said. "But I need to give the people time to mourn before presenting it to my advisors."

"What is it?" I asked.

"I may be able to convince the people to fight for you and your throne...if you marry me," he said.

I looked up into his deep, dark eyes in confusion. "What?"

"Marry me, Sanura," he said. "Be my queen. Then we can take Egypt back for you—together."

I stood up and crossed the room. "No!" I said without even needing time to consider. "Are you crazy? You are not

Egyptian. You cannot be my husband. That would make you pharaoh. You cannot be pharaoh."

"Why not?" Zakai asked, standing up and challenging me. "You think I am not good enough to be your husband?"

"No!" I said, frustrated. "This has nothing to do with you. You forget, I am already promised to Ramses."

"Your brother," Zakai snorted. "Your younger, ineffectual brother. Do you really want to marry him? Can he truly be a better pharaoh than me?"

"It is the Egyptian way," I said. "My place is at my brother's side, as my *father* willed it. It is the marriage my *people* would want. It is the best way to secure peace in Egypt and bring stability to the dynasty. And once I am Ramses's queen, I can bring peace to all of Africa."

Zakai sighed and paced the room for a moment. Then he turned back to me. "I respect that," he finally said. "You and I both understand that we must always do what is best for our people. But..." He hesitated.

"But?" I pushed.

"But my people, my advisors, they will not let me sacrifice more people for a foreign queen," he said. "If you want the strength of my people, we would have to be one united front."

"I could ally with you in another way," I said. "Promise a fair treaty between our nations if I am restored to the throne. But I cannot marry you. No. I will not betray my brother."

Zakai nodded and headed to the door of the hut. But then he stopped and looked at me. "If I were not a king and you were not a queen," he said, "would you marry me?"

"Yes," I said, without hesitation.

He nodded and left the hut. I collapsed onto the bed again. I did not cry, but I slept the sleep of the dead.

11

*O*ver the coming days, as the shock of the attack on the village and the grief over the dead began to subside, the people were less hostile toward me. They still were not overtly friendly, but their scowls and glares softened to uneasy glances and half-hearted smiles. I did my best to stay busy. I helped Tabia with cooking and cleaning and gathering herbs. I attended the eldress's classes for the children and tried to learn some Anwe words. Zakai did not hold it against me that I rejected his marriage proposal. He was busy during the day, meeting with his advisors, but in the evenings, we often took long walks together, talking and laughing as though there was not a huge rift between us. He was a wonderful man, and I knew that I could easily love him. But I would not let my heart admit to something so drastic. It was dangerous, and out of line with my purpose. My only goal was to return to Egypt. I would defeat Keket and resume my place as queen by Ramses's side. Where was the room for Zakai in that future? His place was here, with his own people. With his own queen. I began to wonder if I would simply have to leave Anwe if I hoped to ever return home. I didn't know where I would go, but if the Anwe people would not help me, I would have to find someone else who would.

"Where are we going?" I asked Zakai as he led me by the hand through the village.

"Just wait," he said. "I have something for you."

He took me to the hut that served as an armory. I remembered he had handed me a sword from here when the Egyptian soldiers attacked.

"You said you could fight," Zakai said, leading me inside and holding a torch aloft so I could see. "But you seemed uneasy using the sword."

"I am able to wield a sword," I tried to explain, "but I usually train with an Egyptian khopesh."

Zakai nodded. "I suspected you were more skilled with a different sort of weapon. Here, look around. Choose a weapon you are more comfortable with."

I could not stop the smile from spreading across my face as I surveyed the weapons around me. There seemed to be weapons of every kind here. Many of them were newer, forged here by the Anwe blacksmiths. But others seemed to come from all over the world. Swords of every length and in countless styles. Short and long. Thin and broad. Bronze and steel. Tridents. Spiked balls on chains. Spears. Axes. Bows and arrows. Finally, hidden among the swords, I found a khopesh. It was quite old and needed to be sharpened, but as I held it in my hand, I saw that it was exquisitely made and had excellent balance.

"I will take this to the blacksmith," Zakai said when I showed it to him. "Have him clean it up for you."

"Thank you," I said. "But why are you giving me a weapon?"

He chuckled, that deep rumble that sent a pleasurable shiver down my spine. "My people see it as a sign of friendship." I gave him a cocked eyebrow that told him I didn't believe him. "It's true! It's a symbol of trust, and shows others that I know you will not use it against me."

"It is beautiful," I said, holding the hilt up to the light to admire the craftsmanship.

"You won't be able to walk around the village with it," he said, taking it from me and leading me to the blacksmith's workspace. "You may have noticed that very few people are armed all the time." I nodded. I had noticed. The only people I regularly saw with weapons were the men and women who patrolled the village's boarders. "But you can keep it in your hut so that you can access it easily should we fall under attack again."

Zakai handed the sword to the blacksmith and asked him to sharpen it. The blacksmith sat at a large whetstone and went to work on my new blade.

"Do you think we will come under attack again?" I asked.

"What do you think?" Zakai asked. "How badly does Keket want you?"

I sighed and shook my head. I remembered the sound of her cruel laugh on the wind and the anger on her face when she banished me.

"I don't know," I said. "I only met her a mere days before...before everything happened. And yet, I just have a feeling she wants me dead."

"Then we will be ready for her next time," Zakai said.

When the blacksmith handed me the sword, I did not

feel the sense of pride I had before when I held it. I felt only trepidation.

"I have been wondering," I said as we walked toward my hut, "if I shouldn't leave."

"You want to leave?" Zakai asked, instantly alarmed.

"No," I said. "I don't *want* to leave. But I do not want to bring more death to your people." I didn't tell him that if his people were not going to allow him to help me, I needed to find someone who would. I would have to ease him into the idea of me leaving. If I could even bring myself to do it at all.

"I understand your concerns," Zakai said. "But...if you would only marry me—"

"Zakai..." I grumbled.

"If you would marry me," he continued, "the people would see you as one of us—as Anwe—and they would do whatever it took to protect you."

"I am Egyptian," I said.

"You can be both," he countered.

I shook my head. He would never understand my position. We were in front of my hut, and I squeezed the hilt of my sword in annoyance while looking down at the sand.

"You need to come up with a new plan," I said finally. "Marriage is off the table."

"I am trying to come up with an alternative," he said. "I have been speaking with everyone. My advisors. The shaman. My mother." He sighed and rubbed his forehead.

"And what have they been saying?" I asked.

"My mother thinks that allying with you is good politics," he said. "But the others...they need more of an incentive to help you."

"I understand," I said. "I have nothing to offer you or your people, and even if I did, I would still be asking you to go up against one of the strongest armies in the world."

"I would do anything for you, Sanura," Zakai said. "But I am not one man. I am made up of hundreds of people who comprise my village. I have to take every single one of them into account."

If anyone loved their people more than I did, it was Zakai. Perhaps he did understand me, but he was as trapped as I was. Neither of us was able to move forward.

"Zakai—" I started to say, but I was interrupted by the sound of screams. We looked toward the edge of the village and saw several children running. Zakai and I went to the children, as did several other people.

The children nearly crashed into us in their haste to escape from whatever had been pursuing them. Zakai asked them what was wrong, but all they could do was scream and point, unable to give a clear answer. The parents ran over to collect their children, but one mother could not find her daughter.

"Kaya?" she yelled. "Kaya?"

One of the other children pointed in the direction they came from.

"Take the children," I said to Zakai. "I will find her!"

"No," he said. "You don't know what is out there. I will go."

"I have the sword!" I said, raising my newly sharpened khopesh as I turned and ran out into the grassland.

"Kaya!" I called out as I ran, doing my best to follow the trail left by the children. I heard a scream and ran toward it. Finally, I found Kaya. She was on the ground, trying to crawl away from...what I could only describe as bones wrapped in burial cloth. A mummy. But it was walking. Grunting. It held a sword up above Kaya and moved to strike her. I jumped next to the mummy, using the hook of the khopesh to grab at the mummy's blade, throwing off its attack.

"Run!" I screamed to the girl, gesturing toward safety. "Get back to the village."

The little girl hesitated, but she finally scrambled to her feet and scurried away.

"Who are you?" I asked the creature. "What are you?"

The creature turned its head to me. I could not say it looked at me since it had no eyes, only thick flaps of dried skin where its eyes should be. The muscles and tissue were dried out as well. As a fully mummified corpse, the creature should not be able to move. I could see the straw that had been stuffed inside it to help the body keep its shape after the organs had been removed sticking out between its ribs. I could not deny what I was seeing with my own eyes. The mummy growled as it raised its sword toward me. But it moved slowly and awkwardly. It hacked at me rather than with any sort of skill. I easily dodged its attacks, then I used my own sword to cut off the arm holding the sword. The mummy looked down at its missing limb as though confused. It then tried to pick up the sword with its other arm, but I quickly detached that arm as well.

"Speak, wicked creature!" I commanded. "Were you sent by Keket? How? What is the source of her power?"

The creature looked at me, and the thin papery skin of its mouth stretched into something like a smile. It lunged at me head-first, but I managed to hold it at a distance by impaling it through the chest. The creature continued to growl and kick its legs. I pulled my sword free and then swung around, removing the head from the neck. At that, the skeleton crumpled to the ground.

I was panting, trying to make sense of what happened when Zakai ran to my side.

"What happened?" he asked. "What was it?"

"That," I said, motioning toward the pile of bones.

"What?" he asked, looking at the ancient corpse.

"Exactly," I said. "This mummy is what attacked the children."

"They kept saying something about a 'skeleton man,'" he said, shaking his head. "But I couldn't make sense of it. You are saying that this...this thing that was already dead was walking and scared the children?"

I picked up the short sword the mummy had been carrying and handed it to Zakai. "It did more than walk," I said. "It attacked me with this."

"You cannot be serious," he said, taking the sword gingerly. "We are not really talking about Keket raising the dead?"

"Why not?" I asked as I looked out over the grassland for any signs of more mummies. "We speak of talking lions and armies being transported across the desert. Why not reanimated corpses?"

We walked back to the village, both of us lost in thought, trying to puzzle out what it all meant. Did Keket really have the ability to raise the dead? How was it possible? How was any of this possible?

When we arrived back in the village, the people surrounded Zakai, pressing him for answers. I stepped away, giving him space to comfort them and give them direction. I was standing to one side when I felt a hand on my shoulder. I turned and saw Tabia, motioning for me to follow her. She led me to a hut I had not been to before. As we entered, I realized it was the hut of the shaman.

There was a large fire in the center of the room, and the smoke was wafting out through a hole in the ceiling. The shaman was walking around the fire, tossing items into it and uttering phrases I did not understand. Tabia motioned for me to sit down next to her by the fire. The shaman tossed some herbs onto the fire that caused it to change from red and orange to blue and purple. The flame sparked and the heat made sweat bead on my skin. The smoke swirled around us. I began to feel afraid I would choke on the thick air. I started to stand back up to leave and get some fresh air, but Tabia grabbed my arm and urged me to stay. She motioned with her hand that I should breathe deeply. I did so, and immediately, I felt as though I was flying.

I left Anwe village and flew home. Back to Egypt! I was so happy, I could sing. But as I approached, what I saw nearly left me in tears.

The city was in ruins. The people were in chains. Large beast-like men used whips to force the people to work on a colossal tower dedicated to Keket. All around Luxor was a massive graveyard where the bodies of the dead were tossed and burned without any funerary rites.

I flew up to the top of the tower and saw Keket. She was wearing a pharaoh's helmet. I saw my brother in a cage, forced to beg for food and drink. And behind her throne, I saw the heads of three massive lions on pikes.

I nearly screamed as I forced myself to wake up from the vision.

"No!" I yelled. I looked over and saw that Tabia was with me, as was the shaman. "I...where was I? What happened?"

"What did you see?" the shaman asked.

I told him my vision, the images still vivid in my mind. The shaman sat listening, nodding his head until I finished.

"That is what will come if Keket is allowed to continue her reign of destruction," the shaman said.

"Wait, you can...speak my language?" I asked him.

"I can speak all languages," he said.

"Then why did you not speak to me before now?" I asked. "I could have used someone to talk to besides Zakai."

"I was observing you," the shaman explained. "Getting to know you. Learning if you were worthy of our aid."

"And?" I asked him. "What did you decide?"

He sighed. "You will need for more help than what we can offer you."

I was about to ask him what he meant when Zakai entered the hut.

"What's going on?" he asked.

"The shaman and Tabia helped me see a vision of what is to come if Keket is not stopped," I said, getting to my feet. "We must do something."

"What did you see?" he asked.

"So much death and destruction," I said. "She...It is as if all she wants is to be queen of a graveyard. She has so much anger, such hate in her. She wants to take her revenge out on everyone, not just me."

"I don't know what we can do—" he started to say, but then Tabia and the shaman started speaking to him in their own language. They went back and forth, each trying to explain their case to the others.

"What are they saying?" I asked.

Zakai sighed and translated for me. "They want me to reach out to Oringo and Saleem, the other lion kings."

"Maybe that is a good idea," I said.

Zakai shook his head. "It's a terrible idea. We may all be sons of the Lion Queen, but we have never agreed on anything."

"There is no stronger unifying force than a shared enemy," I said. "If Keket continues down this path of destruction, it won't be long before she comes for them as well. I'm sure of it."

Zakai paced and rubbed his head as he considered this. Tabia spoke to her son again, and the shaman agreed with whatever she told him. Finally, Zakai nodded.

"Very well," he said. "I will send for King Oringo and King Saleem. But I make no promises, Sanura."

I ran to him and threw my arms around his neck. "That is all I can ask."

As we hugged, I could sense his hesitation. I knew he didn't think this would work. In truth, I did not know if there was any way to defeat a sorceress as powerful as Keket.

But we had to try.

12

*Z*akai sent emissaries with letters of invitation to King Saleem of the Nuru people, a desert tribe, and King Oringo of the Dakari people, who lived in a mountainous jungle, immediately. Saleem was quick to respond that he would attend the meeting. But Oringo held the emissary for days before finally agreeing to attend as well. Zakai's people then spent many anxious days preparing huts for two more kings and plenty of food and lodgings for the huge entourages the men would certainly bring with them.

The morning of the meeting, Zakai was seated on a throne in the center of the village. To his right sat his mother, Tabia. To his left, the shaman. I was instructed to stand beside the shaman. All of the villagers lined the path leading to the edge of the village.

Zakai had asked me to say as little as possible earlier that morning as a girl braided my hair. I did not have a proper wig, but I thought it was important that I look as Egyptian as possible for our guests. So, one of the young village girls who was exceptionally skilled at braiding and beadwork agreed to prepare my hair for me that morning. Tabia provided me with a long red dress. I used the key Zakai had given me when I first arrived and opened the lacquered box next to my bed and donned the gold earrings and bangles I had been wearing when I was banished. My heart danced when I put them on. As the only things I had from my homeland, wearing them again brought me great comfort.

I tried not to say anything, insulted by his request, as I finished dressing, but I could hold my tongue no longer.

"Please," Zakai practically begged as he kneeled by my side. "You don't know these men. You don't know our history together. Let me do the talking. If we wish to have any hope of them joining us, please don't say anything."

I turned away from him and looked at my face in the mirror. I ground up some kohl and mixed it with coconut oil to paint my eyes.

"Very well. I want this meeting to be a success even more than you do," I said. "I will do as you ask."

He sighed in relief and kissed my hand. "Thank you, Sanura."

Now, as we waited for Oringo and Saleem to arrive, I was so nauseous with anticipation I did not think I could speak if I wanted to.

Finally, we heard trumpets sound and could see the dust rising from the shuffling of countless feet. The procession for King Saleem had arrived.

At the head of the procession were two rows of ten camels, each one carrying an important looking man in colorful robes. Behind them were a dozen chair bearers carrying women who wore long robes and veils over the lower half of their faces. After that, were countless men carrying the household goods the king and his traveling companions would need for their journey and stay in Anwe village. They also brought crates of chickens and ducks and a herd of goats with them. Finally, King Saleem himself, riding a white horse, approached Zakai.

Saleem dismounted his horse and gave a polite— though not quite as deep as it should have been—bow to Zakai.

I would not know that Saleem was a king if I met him any other place, he was dressed so simply. His robe was plain white, and he wore a white headscarf tied with a simple black cord around the crown of his head. He had a very short and well-manicured mustache and beard. He had gentle brown eyes and a prominent nose. His lips seemed to naturally turn up into a slight smile, as though he was remembering a joke from a long time ago. There was not a single wrinkle marring his olive colored skin. He looked quite young, perhaps only in his early twenties.

He was quite handsome. I noticed that many other young ladies thought so as well as he placed his fists on his hips and looked around the village square where so many people had gathered. When his eyes fell on me, my heart skipped a beat and I felt my face blush. I quickly looked away, looking at the stern face of Zakai. For some reason, I felt guilty even looking at Saleem.

"May the king of the Anwe and our friendship last for one thousand years," Saleem said to Zakai.

Zakai stood and approached Saleem, offering him a hand of friendship. The two men shook, and if Zakai had not told me that there was animosity between them, I never would have known.

"You remember my mother, Tabia," Zakai said.

Saleem bowed to Tabia. "A joy to see you again, my lady," he said.

Zakai then motioned to the shaman. "My chief advisor." Saleem bowed to him as well. Zakai then held a hand out to me. I stepped forward and took it, and offered Saleem a polite curtsey.

"This is Sanura, the rightful queen of Egypt," Zakai said.

"Your Majesty," Saleem said, looking deep into my eyes. My breath hitched in my throat and I was frozen in place. I could not speak or even point out his impertinence in staring at me as well as not bowing. Finally, Saleem looked down, giving me a proper sweeping bow.

"Your Majesty," I managed to stammer back, which came out as a husky whisper.

"So, the 'rightful' queen?" Saleem said to me and Zakai. "I take that to mean you believe there to a usurper in Egypt? Is this why you called me here?"

Zakai clapped Saleem on the back and motioned to a chair beside Tabia. "We will discuss everything once our other guest arrives."

"I was not told who else was attending by your emissary," Saleem said. "Who is coming?"

I saw Zakai hesitate and I wondered why he would not tell Saleem that Oringo—the other lion king—would be present.

"Oringo should be arriving at any moment," Zakai said as he tried to hustle Saleem to his seat, but Saleem went rigid, refusing to be moved.

"What?" Saleem demanded. I thought it would be impossible for Saleem to look angry. His face was as gentle as they come. But the stern intensity of his eyes bored through Zakai, and I could feel the heat of his gaze even though he wasn't looking at me at all.

"Forgive me, brother," Zakai said softly, "for not telling you earlier—"

"Don't you dare call me brother," Saleem hissed. "You know what he did. You know I vowed never to speak to him again. How could you betray me like this?"

I suppressed the urge to get involved and help cool the situation. As much as I wanted to step in and help, I remembered Zakai's words begging me not to get involved. But I hovered on the edge of my toes, ready to jump in should Saleem try to leave.

Zakai and Saleem argued back and forth, with Saleem hurling accusations and Zakai trying to defend himself, when the sound of drumming reached my ears. We all looked back toward the village entrance at what sounded like a great celebration approaching. There was singing and much cheering.

Saleem grunted and shook his head. Oringo was approaching. He would not be able to leave now. I wondered if Zakai had timed their arrivals so perfectly on purpose. If Oringo had arrived first, Saleem would have known and could have turned around and left before ever entering the village. Or if Saleem had arrived too early, someone would have told him that Oringo was coming and he could have slipped back out before Oringo arrived. As it was, he could not leave without imparting a great insult on Zakai and perhaps looking cowardly in the presence of Oringo. Saleem finally took his place beside Tabia, who patted his leg consolingly, but I could not hear or understand her words.

Oringo's people entered the village, all dressed in grass skirts and carrying drums, rattles, and cymbals. They were painted in tribal symbols and had smiles on their faces as they danced down the path to the center of the village.

After the dancers and musicians, nearly a hundred warriors entered, marching in straight lines and chanting.

They wore plumed helmets and carried shields as tall themselves and spears twice as tall.

Finally, Oringo himself entered on the back of a wilde-beest. I had never in my life seen a tamed wildebeest, and indeed, the animal looked as though he would buck Oringo off at the slightest provocation.

Oringo climbed down from the beast and approached. He was bare-chested, with the fur of a silverback gorilla draped over his shoulders. His arms, chest, and obliques were tattooed in tribal symbols. Covering his lower half was a knee-length skirt of embellished leather and knee-high leather boots. He wore a broadsword sheathed to one side. His chin was held high, and his head cocked to one side. He had the bearing of someone who was only here because it amused him, but he could just as easily be anywhere else. His hair was worn in short twists, some of which fell rakishly over his forehead. His skin was like dark mahogany with a slight reddish tinge to it. He had full lips and a broad nose. His eyes surveyed the scene and when he saw me, he winked. For the second time today, I blushed, and then felt guilty for doing so.

"King Zakai," Oringo finally said. He held his arms out and bowed, but even though he performed it correctly, it came across mockingly. "I have answered your call. For what have you summoned me?"

I liked that he was a man who got to the point, but he was ignoring all patterns of respect and diplomacy. However, Zakai seemed used to dealing with Oringo and did not let the young man's impertinence phase him.

"King Oringo," Zakai said. "I am sure you remember my mother, Tabia."

"I do," Oringo said, giving her a nod, but not the bow she deserved.

"And my shaman and chief advisor," Zakai continued.

Oringo only gave the holy man a wave.

"And...I would like to introduce you to Queen Sanura of Egypt," Zakai then said, placing his hand on my lower back.

"Damn," Oringo said slowly as he looked at me from the top of my head to the toes of my feet. "I didn't know you got married, Zakai. You know I would have come for that."

"I'm not Zakai's queen," I corrected. "I am the queen of Egypt."

Oringo chuckled and took my hand, kissing the back of it, never taking his eyes off of mine. "That's good to know, Queen Sanura."

My stomach clenched as he said my name and I thought my knees might give way beneath me. But then Oringo stood quickly and turned back to Zakai.

"But my sources inform me that Egypt has a new young pharaoh," Oringo said. "And he has a very powerful witch by his side. And that his sister—who I assume is Sanura—is a wanted murderess."

People within hearing distance, a mix of Saleem's, Oringo's, and Zakai's people, gasped. I could almost feel the murmur that rippled through the crowd. While Zakai had told his people about Keket, he had not told them the accusations about me killing my father. If people thought I was a killer, that would make convincing them to follow me even more difficult. But there would be no containing that information now.

Zakai's jaw went rigid in frustration at Oringo. But Oringo did not seem flustered in the slightest. I quickly understood that Oringo's main weapon was provocation. By frustrating his enemy, the enemy would lash out in anger, making foolish mistakes. I would have to be careful to make sure I did not let Oringo get under my skin.

I noticed that Oringo still had not addressed Saleem, and that Saleem had hardly moved the whole time. He simply glared at Oringo, his jaw clenched, his eyes hard, his nostrils flaring with each breath. I wondered what Oringo had done to enrage Saleem so completely, but I knew better than to ask. I would find out eventually.

"Please," Zakai finally said, motioning toward Saleem, "do greet our other guest as well."

The whole village seemed to hold their breath. Saleem and Oringo stared at each other. Oringo took his time examining Saleem, and I could tell he was looking for the most direct strike.

"King Saleem," Oringo said without bowing. "Hmm. The moniker of king suits you."

At that, Saleem let out a roar and leapt from his seat. Everyone screamed and jumped back, including me! I thought that Saleem was going to transform into a lion and rip Oringo apart, but Oringo seemed not at all concerned. He laughed and assumed a defensive stance. Zakai jumped between them, grabbing Saleem and looking into his normally placid eyes.

"Don't let him provoke you," Zakai said. "Keep your lion under control."

Zakai's words made my heart race. Was it possible for the lion kings to lose control of the lion half of themselves? When Zakai had been in his lion form, he seemed completely...normal? Human? Either way, I had trusted him. Had been alone with him. Had ridden on his back. Perhaps I should be more cautious around him. Around *all* of them.

Zakai held Saleem back and said some things to him in a low voice to get him to calm down. Eventually, he stopped snarling and trying to attack Oringo—who only stood aside laughing at the scene—and turned away from Zakai, pacing to calm himself down.

I couldn't understand how telling Saleem that "king" was a good moniker for him could be an insult, but Zakai had been right about me not understanding their history together. Whatever Oringo's little jibe meant, it had clearly hit its mark as intended.

"Come," Zakai said, "King Saleem, King Oringo, Queen Sanura, follow me inside where we may talk more privately." He then motioned toward the large hut where he usually held official business. Oringo headed toward the hut first. Then Zakai led Saleem to the hut. I followed the three of them, suppressing the urge to roll my eyes the whole way. For some reason, I thought this would be easier.

Zakai took his seat on the throne and I stood next to him. Oringo and Saleem each faced us, with plenty of room between them.

"The reason I have called you together," Zakai said, "is because we face a common threat."

"Egypt has always tried to provoke conflict," Oringo said. "But they do not pose any real threat to the Dakari, or any African tribe."

"That might have been true in the past," Zakai said. "But that was before Keket. The woman you called a witch."

"Witch. Magician. Sorcerer," Oringo said. "The Egyptians collect magic practitioners like sand."

"True," I said, speaking up. I knew that Zakai wanted me to hold back, but who could explain the Egyptian people and the current threat there better than me? "But our traditional magic practitioners are little more than conjurors. Court jesters. Some invoke the powers of the gods, but none use their powers for evil. Not like Keket."

"Who is this woman?" Saleem asked calmly.

"I don't know," I hated to admit. "I found her in the market. A slave girl who was being abused by her master. I saved her from him and took her into my household. The next day, my father, Pharaoh Bakari, lost his mind. He attacked me and killed my teacher, Habibah. He accidentally fell to his death. And then, somehow, Keket used her powers to transport me here, all the way across the desert. I would have died if Zakai had not found me."

"My condolences on your losses," Saleem said, placing his hand on his heart. "But I still fail to see what this has to do with any of us. Problems in Egypt have never been our concern."

"Last week," Zakai explained, "we were attacked by Egyptian soldiers."

"Here?" Oringo asked, for the first time showing concern.

"Yes," Zakai said. "Keket imbued the men with preternatural speed. They were able to cross the desert much faster and easier than normal men. Without my lion form, I never would have been able to stop them."

Oringo and Saleem both crossed their arms as they considered this information, each carefully contemplating his response.

"So why bring us together?" Oringo asked. "Did you think we would all join hands and fight together against Keket?"

"Something like that," Zakai said evenly. "If Keket's forces can reach us here, they can reach you as well."

"They are still Egyptians," Oringo said, his chest puffing up. "We have fought them off for centuries. Let them come."

"It would be in everyone's best interest to stop Keket and reinstall Sanura to her rightful place," Zakai said.

"Wait," Saleem said. "Forgive me, my lady, but defeating

an enemy would be completely different from installing another one."

"I am not your enemy—" I tried to say, but Saleem continued.

"I would respectfully point out that you are," he said. "For centuries there have been hostilities between Egypt and the rest of Africa. It would be in all of our best interests for Egypt to fall."

I was shocked into silence. I couldn't believe that Saleem was suggesting such a thing as to let Egypt, a symbol of peace and stability in the world, to collapse.

"Would it not be more beneficial to have a power such as Egypt as an ally?" Zakai pointed out, for which I was grateful.

Saleem shrugged. "The Nuru would be more than happy to take our chances without the Egyptians."

My shock quickly gave way to anger. Egypt had been in existence for more than two thousand years! How could he so willfully and flippantly wish for the end of my people? Our culture? Our traditions?

Oringo laughed. "Wow, Saleem," he said. "For a desert dweller, that's cold. But for once, I agree with you."

Zakai shot Oringo a look. "You would also prefer Egypt to fall?"

"I'd like to be the one to drag it down myself," he said. And he seemed not to care about the pain his words caused me. "I have an army at my disposal. If Egypt is weak, I say we march on Luxor and take the palace and the throne for ourselves."

"No!" I yelled. "You cannot do that. The people would never accept you. The throne is mine!"

Oringo chuckled and I realized I had easily fallen into his trap.

"You show your true colors, *Queen* Sanura," he said. "Is this about protecting Africa? Or about making you queen?"

I stammered, trying to come up with a response, but I caught a look from Zakai, warning me not to speak. I sighed and looked away in embarrassment.

"Egypt in its current state is a danger to all of Africa," Zakai said. "In order to survive, we need to band together. Form an alliance. We can decide the fate of Egypt, and Queen Sanura, later."

"The Dakari have never needed the Anwe to survive," Oringo declared. "And we aren't going to start now. If Egypt must fall, let it. I don't care."

"And you forget one other thing," Saleem added. "The Nuru will never form an alliance with the Dakari under Oringo." He nearly spat Oringo's name as though it was dirt on his tongue.

Oringo laughed. "Well, I think we know where we all stand. I'm hungry." With that, he stood and left the tent without properly excusing himself.

Saleem grimaced and touched his forehead, then his heart, and then bowed before seeing himself out.

"That went about as well as I expected," Zakai said, slumping into his throne and rubbing his forehead.

"That was terrible," I said. "They did not agree to...to anything. Not even further talks. They would rather Luxor burn to the ground than help me. What are we going to do?"

Zakai stood up and shook his head. "I don't know," he said. "But I knew that they would never join an alliance. I only hosted this talk for your benefit."

"No wonder you failed," I spat. "You went into this expecting failure. You lost before the battle was even waged!"

"Sanura," he said reaching out for me, but I pulled away. "This is not Egypt. This is Africa. Things are different here. And we are not mere men. We are lion shifters. That complicates matters. We will never be able to work together —even if it would be to the benefit of all."

"I don't accept that," I said, turning away to leave the tent.

"Where are you going?" he asked.

"To get my alliance," I said.

13

*Z*akai and I and the people of Anwe had all hoped that after the three lion kings met, we would have at least the beginnings of a possible alliance, and that we would then spend the evening in celebration. When I left the hut, the mood in the village was anything but celebratory. The three tribes, instead of intermingling, were divided. Saleem's people took up residence around the hut we had arranged for him on the western side of the village. Zakai's people were quiet and going about their business as usual, not intermingling with the guests. The only sound came from outside the village, in the grasslands, where Oringo's people had set up camp on their own, eschewing the huts we had prepared for them. I could hear music and laughter coming from their camp, so I decided to go and see Oringo first. I had a feeling that Saleem would be more easily convinced to join the alliance than Oringo, so there was no point in talking to Saleem until I could persuade Oringo over to our side.

The day was already turning into twilight, and the Dakari had started a huge bonfire in the middle of the camp, along with various small fires set up closer to the tents. Guards with shields and spears stood every few feet around the perimeter of the camp. When I entered the camp, the smell of roasted meat immediately wafted to my nose, along with the scent of strong spices. People who were not cooking or eating or standing guard were sitting around the fire singing, clapping, beating drums, and shaking rattles. The people all watched me as I walked through the camp, but no one tried to speak with me—until I reached Oringo's tent. Two guards crossed their spears in front of me.

"State your business," one of the men said.

"I wish to speak with King Oringo," I said.

"I will see if the king wishes to speak with you," the man replied before ducking inside. I crossed my arms and waited. I had no doubt that Oringo would see me. Making me wait was just for show. Just another way to prove his power over the situation.

The guard came back and both of them moved their spears aside.

"The king will see you," the guard said.

"How magnanimous of him," I grumbled as I stepped through the flap. I coughed as I entered the tent, my lungs almost instantly filled with pungent smoke. I waved my hand in front of my face to clear the smog. "What the..." I mumbled as my vision cleared.

Oringo was sitting on a chair being handed a long silver pipe by a scantily clad woman. As I looked around, I noticed that there were many beautiful, nearly naked women present. The ground was covered with many animal skins and there was a large bed made up of furs.

"My queen," Oringo called out, his smile wide. He held

open his arms and beckoned me to him. "To what do I owe the pleasure of your visit?"

"Can we speak in private?" I asked him.

"I am sure that anything you have to say to me you can say in front of my lovely harem," he said with a chuckle. Some of the women around us giggled as well.

"How many women do you need to prove your virility?" I asked disdainfully, looking at the women as though they bored me. "Most men only need one."

Oringo took a long drag on his pipe and regarded me. I must have measured up to his qualifications because he clapped his hands and the women all languidly sauntered out of the room, but not without a few disdainful looks my way. Oringo stood and walked over to a low couch. He sat on it and motioned for me to sit next to him.

"Please," he said.

I went to the couch, but sat on the opposite end, as far away from him as possible. He gave a slow nod and then offered me a pipe one of the women left behind. I shook my head.

"I need my wits about me," I said.

Oringo took another pull from his own. "I doubt anything could dull your senses," he said. "You were relatively quiet in that meeting with Zakai, but I think you are far more clever than you let on. Like a cat, am I right? Isn't that what 'Sanura' means?"

I nodded, impressed that he had taken the time to learn what my name meant, although I'm not sure how he had discovered it so quickly.

"Why won't you even entertain the idea of an alliance?" I asked him.

"Because I don't need Zakai for anything," he said. "The Dakari don't need anyone."

"This isn't about Zakai," I said. "It is about what is best for all of Africa."

"And you think *you* are what is best for Africa," he said. A statement, not a question, but I did not reply. "What do you even know about Africa? Before you got banished, had you ever even left Luxor?"

"I don't need to leave Luxor to know that I am a better option for everyone than Keket," I said.

"How do you know that?" Oringo challenged. "You said you don't know her. What are her goals? Her objectives? Maybe Egypt needs a change. Toss out those stuffy pharaohs and conjurors with their silly tricks and do something positive for once."

"Keket is evil!" I said more forcefully than I meant to. "She killed my father."

"So?" he said. "Sometimes death is necessary. You'd kill Keket if given the chance, wouldn't you?" Again, I didn't answer. "Keket has a goal, and she killed to reach that end. I'd do the same. I've *done* the same. If you don't have it in you to make the hard choices, you don't deserve to be queen."

"I am queen," I said, sitting up even straighter.

Oringo chuckled. "Yeah, a queen without a kingdom."

I can't explain why, but his words stung. I looked away so he would not see my eyes water. He was right, unfortunately. I had been banished and I couldn't return. My own brother thought I had killed our father. My own soldiers had kidnapped me and tried to take me back to Egypt in a cage. What was a queen without her people?

"But I can change that for you," Oringo said. He reached over and ran a finger down my arm, sending a chill like ice through my veins and I shivered. I looked back at him and felt my stomach quiver as I looked into his eyes.

"You'll join our alliance?" I asked, hope clear in my voice.

Oringo laughed out loud, a full-throated laugh he had to toss his head back to fully release.

"No, my dear," he said. "But I'll marry you. Make you my queen. Then, together, you and I, along with my people, we can wage war on Egypt together. We can overthrow Keket and claim the throne there, too. Just like that, we'd have an empire. How does Empress Sanura sound?"

"No," I said without hesitating. I did not want to be empress. I had no desire to conquer Africa like my father did. All I wanted was what was rightfully mine. By blood. By inheritance. By marriage. I would be queen of Egypt—nothing more, nothing less.

"I'm not sure you've really thought this through, kitten," Oringo said. "How do you plan to take Egypt without my help?"

"I don't. I need you," I admitted. "I need your army. I need your lion. I need the support of your people."

"Then how do you plan to get it?" he asked.

"I don't know," I said. "But I will."

Oringo stretched and took another long drag from his pipe as though he were bored of me. "I have given you my terms," he said. "Marry me and be my queen. Otherwise, I will overthrow Egypt on my own and name myself pharaoh."

I stood and walked out of the tent, with the sound of Oringo's laugh in my wake.

It was now fully dark. As I walked through the village, all of Oringo's people seemed to be laughing at me as they danced, drank, and smoked. Out of the corner of my eye I saw Oringo's women go back into his hut. For some reason, seeing those women go to him made me angry. No, it wasn't anger. It was jealousy. Though I couldn't figure out why. He was attractive, yes. But he was also offensive. He was a brute who only wanted battle and bloodshed. He wanted me as his wife to add to his harem as a trophy. He didn't respect me as a queen. As a woman. As his equal. I could never love a man like that.

Love? Ugh. I scoffed to myself as I left the camp and went out into the grasslands to clear my head, which had been made fuzzy from the smoke. What was *I* doing thinking about love? I wouldn't marry for love, and even if I did, I'd marry Zakai. Anyway, there was no use dwelling on it. When I married, it would be for stability and political advantage. Marriage to Zakai or Oringo could possibly give me a military advantage for now, but neither would provide Egypt with stability in the long run. If anything, such a union could undermine any gains I made. The people would not accept a foreign king or pharaoh. No. I still had to marry Ramses. Love did not factor into the equation.

I think Zakai and Oringo were messing with my head. I had spent many years studying strategy with Chike and Habibah, but I had not spent much time actually putting what I had learned into practice. This was my first real attempt at forming a military alliance and I was failing miserably.

I looked out into the grasslands and saw the many glowing eyes staring back at me. I felt a shiver. How long did we have before Keket sent something else to attack us? That mummy she sent was probably only a test. It must have taken great power to raise the dead. I had defeated it easily, but it was slow and clumsy and alone. If Keket somehow managed to raise a great number of mummies, we could all be in grave danger.

I went back into the village. As I walked, I felt everyone's eyes on me. And even though I could not understand them, I knew they were talking about me. They were not happy that Zakai had kept the details of my past a secret from them. And I knew that they would not want to take up arms against Egypt on my behalf. Oringo had insulted all of the Anwe, and he had come here at my request. At this point, I doubted that even if I did marry Zakai his people would willingly fight for me.

I found myself back in front of Zakai's hut, but I couldn't bring myself to go in. I told him that I was going to go and get an alliance, but I had failed. I couldn't face him. I had not spoken to Saleem yet, but I had a feeling I would not succeed there either. I needed help. But who could I turn to? Everyone I had ever relied on was dead or a thousand miles away. Anat. Father. Habibah. Chike. I looked up at the night sky and could not even see the stars above from all the fires in the village.

I went back to the healing hut for a moment of solitude to think before I approached Saleem. I sat on my bed and rubbed my face with my hands. I then cursed to myself when I realized I had smudged my makeup. I grunted in annoyance and went to the dressing table and looked at myself in the mirror. I used a rag to clean my smudged face and then fixed the kohl around my eyes. As I looked at myself, my eyes drifted to the altar of the three lion skulls. The one person who was still with me—who was always with me—was Sekhmet.

I explored the healing hut for items I could use in a prayer ritual to invoke Sekhmet and request her aid. I found candles, orange and red crystals, and a great variety of herbs. I also grabbed my khopesh, which I had placed near the door in case I ever needed to grab it quickly. I placed the stones on the lion skulls and then around them. I placed two candles in front of the altar and lit them. I then lit the herbs and wafted the smoke around the altar and myself. I placed my khopesh before the altar. I kneeled and folded my hands in front of me. I raised my eyes to the lion skulls and spoke loudly and clearly.

"Oh, Sekhmet, Goddess of war, of blood. Goddess of healing and the desert wind. Mother of lions. Hear my plea."

I thought I felt a slight breeze on my feet and shoulders, but when I looked toward the door, the flap was still closed. I turned back to the altar.

"Beloved Sekhmet, she who overcomes all enemies, I call upon you now to conquer the fear and uncertainty in my heart. Give me strength of heart, of soul, and of mind."

The temperature in the room seemed to rise, and the candles burned brighter.

"Goddess Sekhmet, let no one intimidate me nor bar my way. If I am not worthy of your aid, please show me the way of honor."

I picked up the khopesh and dragged it along the palm of my hand, crying out as I cut the skin and let the blood flow. Sekhmet was a warrior goddess and she needed a gift of blood to know that I was earnest. I stood and squeezed my hand into a fist, letting drops of blood drip onto each lion skull.

Suddenly, a great wind like a cyclone filled the room, along with an intense heat. I tried to look around, fearful that the hut was on fire, but the sand and wind burned my eyes. I cried out and fell to my knees before the altar.

"Sekhmet!" I called out. "Hear me! Forgive my weakness and fill me with your power!"

I heard a great roar of a lion and the room went black and still.

I am with you, a voice whispered.

When I opened my eyes, the candles were burning normally and there was no wind. The room was not overly hot. I looked at my hand and saw that there was no wound. The blood on the lion skulls was gone. I sighed in relief, hoping that Sekhmet had accepted my offering and would lend me her strength. I supposed the only way I would know if I had the strength of the lion goddess was to do what needed to be done and succeeded.

I placed my khopesh back by the door and walked to Saleem's hut.

14

The difference in the atmosphere between Saleem's people and Oringo's people was striking. Saleem's people chose to stay in the huts and tents provided by Anwe village, and even though there were many people here, they were rather quiet. They were talking and laughing, but their voices were kept low and they were not playing music. The men were all dressed similarly, in long white robes and headscarves. The women, however, wore a bright variety of colors and their headscarves were all different styles. Some wore scarves over only their hair, some covered their faces, and some did not wear head coverings at all. Everyone gave me a polite smile and nod as I walked through the camp, but no one approached to speak to me.

As I reached Saleem's hut, the guards gave me a polite bow and one of them opened the flap to the hut for me instantly, announcing my name as I entered.

Like Oringo's hut, Saleem's was also filled with women, but they were of various ages and all dressed the same as the women outside. I did not know who the women were, but for some reason, I did not get the feeling that these women were for Saleem's pleasure.

Saleem had been lounging on a pile of pillows, and the room was strewn about with decorative rugs, woven blankets, and sheer mosquito nets. He walked up to me and touched his forehead, then his heart, and then bowed to me.

"Queen Sanura," he said. "You honor me with your visit."

"Thank you for seeing me," I said.

Saleem then motioned for all the ladies to join us. "These are the women of my family. My aunts, cousins, and sisters."

The women all curtseyed and welcomed me in their native language. I smiled and curtseyed back. Relief flooded over me when I realized the women were all his relations and not his personal harem. Saleem did not strike me as the sort of man who would have a herd of women at his beck and call.

"Thank you for your warm welcome," I said, though I had no idea if they understood me.

"To what do I owe the pleasure of your company?" Saleem asked me.

"I was hoping we could speak privately," I said.

"Of course," he said. He spoke to the women in their own language and they all gave him a polite bow and left the hut, leaving us alone. Saleem then invited me to sit on the rug and pillows he had been lounging on earlier. "Can I offer you something to drink?" He picked up a small cup and handed it to me.

"I would prefer not to have any alcohol right now," I said.

He chuckled. "This is not alcohol," he explained, pressing the cup toward me. "Quite the opposite, in fact."

I took the small cup and held it to my nose. The dark brown liquid had a lovely rich aroma. I took a small sip and then made a face.

"Oh," I said, trying not to spit the vile liquid back out. "That...is quite something." It had a heavy, woody flavor that was lacking in its aroma. The aftertaste was not altogether unpleasant, lighter and crisper than the initial gulp, but it was not enjoyable enough for me to want to drink more.

Saleem laughed. "It is an acquired taste, or so I have been told. But I have been drinking it since I was a child."

"What is it?" I asked.

"Coffee," he said. "Originally from Abyssinia. Not far from Egypt. I am surprised it is unknown to you."

"I've never heard of it. We usually prefer tea," I said, placing the cup aside.

"Egypt does have wonderful tea," Saleem said, setting his cup aside as well.

"You have been to Egypt?" I asked, delighted to be able to talk to someone who was familiar with my country.

"Many times," he said. "I was a student of Psamtic."

"You are kidding!" I said. "I know of Psamtic. He and my teacher, Habibah, often disagreed over the interpretations of ancient texts. His death was a great tragedy."

"Indeed, it was. But I have heard of Habibah as well," Saleem said with a smile. "But I never had the pleasure of meeting her myself. I would love the opportunity."

I could feel the smile run away from my face as a pain stabbed my heart, and the grin fell from Saleem's face.

"Did I say something wrong?" he asked.

I shook my head. "No," I said. "You didn't know. But Keket killed Habibah. At least, I think she was responsible."

Saleem furrowed his brow. "What do you mean?"

"My father," I said, "lost his mind. He killed Habibah and attacked me before he fell from a balcony and died. I believe he was under Keket's control."

Saleem nodded slowly as he considered my words, but I had a feeling he was not quite convinced.

"The queen also died recently, did she not?" he asked, and I bristled at the insinuation.

"She did," I said. "But that was many months ago. And my father was acting normally until that fateful night."

"But as you know, from being a pharaoh's daughter, that how we act in public does not always reveal our true feelings," he said. "Perhaps your father was suffering far more than you knew."

I pressed my lips to force myself to think before responding. I did not want to react with emotion. And Saleem had a point. I could see that he was a logical man. An intellectual. He would have to be convinced with reason and evidence.

"That could be true," I said. "But when I looked into his eyes that night, that man was not my father. And when Keket sent her soldiers here to capture me, I saw the same look in their eyes as well. Those men were not in possession of their own thoughts and minds. Keket was controlling them."

"Let's say I believe you," Saleem said, which caused me to suck in a breath. How could he not believe me? But I stayed silent...for the moment. After all, he had not witnessed what Zakai or I had these past days. "What is it you want?"

"I want to return to Egypt and take back my throne," I

said. "Keket is a usurper. She has my brother under her thrall. I need to reclaim what is rightfully mine."

"But how can I help you with that?" he asked.

"You are a lion," I said. "And you are the leader of a large tribe. You have warriors. You could support me."

Saleem shook his head, and I could tell he was trying to keep from rejecting me outright. "I have a tribe, yes, but we are not warriors. My people have suffered great losses. I would not want to cause them more distress."

"But Keket will come for you," I said. "Or Ramses will. My father wanted nothing more than to subjugate the African tribes, but he did not have the means. My brother will fulfill our father's dream, and he has Keket's power behind him. It is only a matter of time before Egypt's armies are at your door."

"Then we will face them when they come, but in our own way," Saleem said. "Diplomacy. Trade. Treaties. Marriages. Alliances. There are many ways to avoid conflict without fighting."

"I was never given the opportunity to explore those options," I said, leaning back on the pillows. "I held Habibah in my arms as she died. I watched my father fall to his death. My brother was taken from me and I was banished from my homeland."

"Sanura—" he tried to say, but I cut him off.

"I lost everything in a mere instant," I said. "And then my own soldiers attacked me. They killed Zakai's people without warning. Keket does not want diplomacy. She wants my head on a platter. She must be stopped."

"Believe it or not," he said as soon as I stopped to take a breath, "I do understand where you are coming from. Do you know why there are so many women here? It is because there are no men. My father, my uncles, my brothers. All of them are dead. And I wasn't there to help them. I only lived because I was away studying. That is why I am king today."

"Then you do understand me," I said, growing hopeful. "You know what it is like to have to carry the blessing and the burden of your family's legacy. I don't do this just for me, but for my father. My brother. My mother. All those pharaohs who came before me."

Saleem reached over and took a strand of my hair in his fingers. He twirled it around thoughtfully. Even though he was not touching my skin, I broke out in gooseflesh as if he had and I did not stop him. Suddenly, I wanted nothing more than for his hands to touch my face, my neck, my shoulders...all of me.

What was happening to me? I was not usually this person. Someone who put any stock into feelings. It seemed as though falling in love with Zakai had opened the floodgates of my heart and now I wanted to love every man I met. Well, not every man. Only the lion kings. Zakai, Oringo, and Saleem.

"What?" I asked. Saleem had said something, but I had not heard him, I was so busy imagining what his touch on my flesh might feel like.

"I asked if you would risk the lives of your people for a man you've only just met?" he repeated.

"Perhaps," I said. "If I thought it would benefit them."

"And what benefit is there for me to support a queen without a kingdom?" he asked. "Without an army? Without even the support of her own people?"

"I will have the support of the people," I said. "I am sure of it. If they were not under Keket's control and able to make their own decisions."

"Do you really believe she has the power to control the minds and hearts of an entire nation?" he asked.

"I don't know what she is capable of," I said. "And I don't want to wait to find out. What I have already seen her do is frightening enough."

"I am sorry, Sanura," he said, letting go of my hair and sighing. "I just don't think I can risk the lives of my people for you...unless..."

"Unless what?" I asked.

"Unless you married me," he said.

I nearly laughed. Not at the idea of marrying Saleem. He seemed like a gentle, loving man who would make a good husband. But that he would propose marriage right after meeting me, just as Oringo had. And only days after Zakai. For all the lion kings liked to talk about their differences, they certainly had the same taste in women. Or in one woman at least.

I did my best to choke back my laughter so as not to hurt his pride. "I'm sorry," I said. "But I can't do that. I am promised to Ramses."

"Your brother?" he asked, raising an eyebrow.

"Yes," I said, irritated that once again I was having to justify what everyone knew was an ancient tradition in my country. "Marriage to Ramses is the best path toward long-term stability in Egypt. The pharaoh and queen must be Egyptian."

"Are you certain of that?" he asked.

"Ramses is already pharaoh," I said. "He became pharaoh the moment my father died. I would never overthrow my brother. My only goal is to rid the court of Keket so I can take my rightful place at his side."

"I am sorry, then," Saleem said as he stood. He offered me a hand to help me stand from the comfortable pillows as well. "But I do not think there is anything you can offer me that would be incentive enough to pledge my troops to your cause."

"I am sorry too," I said, and I truly was. "The time will come when Keket's power threatens the whole of Africa, if not the world. I only hope when that happens, that it will not be too late for you to reconsider."

Saleem pressed his lips. There was nothing more to say. He touched his forehead and his heart and then bowed to me before motioning toward the door. I bowed in return and took my leave. I did not speak to any of his people or family members as I left.

I slowly walked back to Zakai's hut. I was sorely disappointed in Oringo and Saleem, that they could not see the danger that was coming. That they could not overcome their differences enough to band together for the greater good.

But even more so, I was disappointed in myself. My powers of persuasion and diplomacy were profoundly lacking. Habibah and Chike would hang their heads in shame at being associated with me. My father would revoke my title of queen if he could see me now. I was also greatly embarrassed to have to return to Zakai with no alliance. While I did not think he would hold my failure against me, I had been so confident that the men would listen to me more than they had to him. What was I missing? Was I the only person who could truly see how dangerous Keket was? Shouldn't everyone want to band together against her? All of our tribes would be stronger together than standing apart.

What did I just say? "Our" tribes? What was wrong with me? I was not Anwe, or Dakari, or Nuru. I was Egyptian. Even if I never returned to Egypt, I would always be Egyptian.

Before I realized it, I was back in Zakai's hut.

"How did it go?" he asked me. But from the look on his face, I could tell he already knew the answer.

"They both declined to join in any alliance," I said, walking over to a table and pouring myself a glass of wine. I needed it.

Zakai said nothing, but watched me as I crossed the room.

"What?" I asked, exasperated. "Aren't you going to tell me that you told me so?"

"No," he said, walking over to me and rubbing my arms. Then he kissed my forehead tenderly. "Because you already know I did," he whispered.

I laughed and playfully slapped him away, downing my cup of wine quickly and pouring another one.

"So, what do we do now?" I asked, my disappointment clear in my voice.

He wrapped me in his large, protective arms and I relaxed into him. There was no point in fighting him. And I didn't want to. He was the only ally I had. The only friend. The only lover.

"Do not worry for now," he said. "Tonight, you are safe. Tomorrow, we will bid the Dakari and Nuru farewell. Then, we will meet with my advisors and consider a plan moving forward."

"We do not have enough people to launch an attack on Egypt," I said.

"No," he agreed.

"And we were not able to convince Oringo or Saleem to join us," I said.

"No," he agreed again.

"So, it is not likely your advisors are going to support any sort of military action against Egypt," I said.

He pressed his lips and sighed. "True. I am afraid that there is no scenario available to us that will get you what you want."

I pulled away from him, the wine pulsing through my veins and making my cheeks hot. "I'll never give up," I said. "I'll never abandon my people. My brother. I'll never stop fighting for what is rightfully mine!"

He reached for me. "Sanura—" But I pulled away.

"No," I said. "You cannot seduce me into changing my mind. This is serious!"

"You might be serious," Zakai said, his own temper rising. "But you are not seeing reason! You are out of options."

"There has to be a way," I said. "The gods would not abandon me. They would not abandon Egypt. Sekhmet—"

"Sekhmet is a goddess of war," Zakai said. "She *wants* bloodshed. If Keket will bring death, Sekhmet will bless her."

"No," I said. Sekhmet had blessed me! She came to me in the healing hut. She had protected me in the desert. I had prayed to her all of my life and she always led me. She would not betray me for Keket. "I don't believe you."

"I am a son of the Lion Queen," he said. "I know our true nature. I know what it is to crave blood. If Sekhmet is the mother of lions, then she will always give way to her most bestial nature."

"You are lying!" I said.

Zakai's face transformed into something like half lion and half man. Large fangs grew from his mouth and he let out a terrifying snarl. "I never lie!" he roared at me.

I screamed and fell on my backside, the terror of seeing into the face of a beast coursing through me. My eyes were wide and I panted in fear, unable to catch my breath.

All at once, Zakai returned to his human form and he offered his hand to me.

"Sanura!" he gasped. "I'm so sorry. Here, let me help you."

"No," I said, gathering my wits and getting to my feet. "You can't help me."

I ran out of the hut, but where was I to go? I still had no one and nothing. If I ran into the grasslands, I would face untold dangers. I went back to the healing hut, but seeing the altar of Sekhmet brought me no comfort. I went to the altar and one by one, I threw the skulls of lions out of the hut onto the ground, along with the rest of the altar items. When I tossed out the last of the items, many of the Anwe villagers had gathered to see what was wrong with me. Tabia herself was gathering up the lion skulls. She looked at me with disgust on her face, but I didn't care.

"Stay away from me!" I screamed. I threw the flap closed and sat on my bed and fumed. Not for the first time that night, I was disappointed with myself. I had desecrated Tabia's altar. I was sure I would pay for that later. But what did it matter? I had lost everything. My only possession the world was my life. And as far I was concerned, the Anwe could have it.

15

The next day, I woke up later than I had expected to. The sun was already hot. I had hoped to have one more chance to speak with Saleem and Oringo. Maybe, just maybe, they would change their minds. See the coming danger for what it really was and pledge to join forces with Zakai to help me take back my throne.

I dressed quickly, but when I reached the side of the village where Saleem's people had been staying, they were already gone. I cursed to myself and ran to the other end, out into the grasslands, praying that Oringo would still be there. But he was gone as well. I cursed again and remembered my abominable actions from the night before. No wonder the gods were not answering my prayers. I would have to build a new temple to atone for what I had done. But without money or a place to build one, it would be a long time before I had the means to do that.

As I stood alone on the empty field, I wondered what to do next. Part of me did not want to return to Anwe village. I was embarrassed by my actions and had a feeling they would not be keen to help me, or even give me sanctuary. If I had not left the khopesh Zakai had given me back in the hut, I might have simply walked away. If I could not find what I needed here, there was no reason to stay. While the lion kings might have been the most powerful tribal leaders in Africa, they were not the only ones. I could possibly find allies elsewhere. And if I could not find help in Africa, there was a whole world of people out there. Rome. The Middle East. China. As Keket's power grew, she could threaten everyone. No one would be safe no matter how far from Egypt they were. Somewhere out there would be someone who could help me.

But that would mean leaving Zakai. As much as I hated to admit it, I did love him. And I knew that he loved me. And I did not know if I could face what was coming alone. If I left, there was no guarantee I would ever find anyone to help me. Here, at least, I could have a home. A life. For at least a little while. Until Keket came for me.

In spite of the heat, I shivered at the thought of more of Zakai's people dying because of me. In the distance, I could see the graves of those we had already buried. Keket knew where I was. There was no hope in hiding here. Her power —and her army—would grow. And eventually, she would strike again. Zakai and his people were strong, but they could not repel her forever. If I left, at least the Anwe would be safe—for a little while. I had a feeling that Keket would pursue me to the ends of the earth. Then, she would set her sights on everyone else.

"A grain of rice for your thoughts?" I heard Zakai ask. I turned and did my best to give him a smile, but it came across as more of a grimace, so I turned back to the empty grassland. "You weren't planning on going with Oringo, were you?"

"No," I said. "I was just hoping he might listen to reason if I tried one more time."

He stood next to me so I could see him out of the corner of my eye. "I am sorry for losing my temper with you last night."

"But...?" I asked.

"No excuses," he said. "I was out of line."

I was surprised. I expected him to blame me for being unreasonable or blame his lion beast, but he did not. My anger at him melted away and I leaned on his shoulder. He wrapped his arm around me and held me close. For a moment, we stood together in silence. No words were needed.

"I don't think I will ever abandon my dream of returning home," I said.

"I know," he replied. "If I were banished from Anwe, I would never stop trying to return to my people."

I sighed, tears pricking my eyes. "Then what am I to do?" I asked. "I don't want to give up, but I don't see a way forward."

"A new bridge cannot be built in a day," he said, turning me to face him. "You came here, declaring your birthright and forcing a meeting between other tribes, other kings you don't know, and tried to force an alliance. That is not diplomacy. You don't know them. You barely know me. Relationships take time."

I knew he was right. Egypt had been a kingdom for thousands of years. We had built friendship and alliances and enemies over decades, or even centuries. I had watched as my father cultivated the friendships developed by our forefathers by hosting elaborate festivities for visiting dignitaries or sending exquisite gifts.

"But how am I to establish relationships with new allies

now?" I asked. "I don't have decades, or even years, to cultivate such friendships."

"You start here," he said, turning me toward the village. "My people are open to accepting you. But you have held them at a distance. You cannot expect them to fight for you if they do not love you."

I sighed, once again recalling how I threw their altar into the dirt. What was it Habibah had told me? *As long as you have the love of the people, you'll never have to worry a day in your life.* "I acted shamefully," I said, knowing I had failed my teacher.

"As we all do from time to time," he said with a chuckle. "But they will forgive you. You are already one of us, whether you want to be or not. Make allies here, and then your influence will spread."

I sighed and hugged him. I wondered in that moment if he had asked me to marry him again if I would have said yes. I was sorely tempted. How better to seal my relationship with the Anwe more quickly than by becoming their queen? By becoming Anwe? But thankfully, he did not ask. And I did not have to make that decision.

As we started to walk back to the village, I heard a strange humming sound. At first, I thought I was imagining it, but when I looked at Zakai, I saw that he was looking for the source of the sound as well. It reminded me of the sound of thousands of bees. I had once visited at a honey farm outside of Luxor, and I was shocked at the deafening roar that could be made by such tiny creatures when they banded together. But this sound was louder. Deeper. As though there were not just thousands of bees, but millions. And much bigger ones at that.

I saw the people in the village growing concerned as well, collecting their children and running into their huts as a great roaring wind rent the air. And then the sun grew dark. I heard buzzing whoosh past my ear as a large black scarab flew by. Then, I saw another, and another. A swarm of scarabs swirled around us and through the village. We tried to bat them away, but there were too many of them. We ran toward the village, but it grew dark and cold.

Zakai and I looked to the sky, directly into the sun. But it was no longer burning hot and bright. The scarabs flocked together and formed a large black mass in front of the sun, blocking its rays and turning day into night. Then the swirling mass moved together to create the likeness of a face. A face I knew all too well.

"Keket!" I gasped.

The face in the mass laughed. "So, you have not forgotten me, *mistress*," she hissed.

"I think of nothing else!" I yelled back.

"What is happening?" Zakai yelled.

"Silence!" Keket ordered him. "This is between me and Sanura."

"What do you want?" I asked her. "Why are you doing this?"

"It is time for the slaves, the downtrodden, the abused to rise up," Keket said.

"If you had a grievance about the way you were treated," I said, "you could have spoken to me. I saved you from an abusive master, remember?"

"And yet you did not know my name," she said.

"Why do you keep saying that?" I asked her, clenching my jaw and my fists.

"You did not save me for my sake," she said. "You saved me for yours. I could have been anyone. Any nameless, faceless child in the street and you would have done the same thing."

"I saw *you*," I insisted. "I saw you and I helped you."

"And what of the thousands of other slaves in Egypt?" she asked. "The millions around the world? What about them?"

"You are right," I said, and for a moment, I thought the buzzing quieted. "No one should live as a slave. If you allow me to return, we can work this out."

The buzzing then grew louder and the face of Keket bared its teeth. "No," she growled. "I can change the world starting right now. Without you!"

Her mouth then opened and the scarabs poured forth like an ocean wave. Zakai and I ducked and put our arms over our heads as we felt the beetles swarm around us. They engulfed the village, and we heard screams from the people and the mooing of cows and the bleating of goats. The roosters crowed and the dogs howled.

And then there was silence.

The scarabs vanished and the sun was shining brightly again.

Then there was a scream.

Zakai took my hand and we scrambled to our feet, running into the village.

"Chebe!" one little girl was crying over the skeleton of a dog. "The scary cloud lady killed my Chebe!"

I was completely confused. My brain could not process what I was seeing. Why was the child crying over the bones of a dog that had clearly died years ago?

"My goats!" someone else cried.

"My chickens!" another person yelled.

It took me another moment to understand what had happened, but then it was horrifyingly clear. Keket had sent the beetles to kill and strip the flesh from the bones of every animal in the village.

"This is impossible!" Zakai exclaimed, but as we explored the entire village, we knew it was true. The people then crowded around Zakai in the village center in a panic. The beetles had killed all the animals, most of which were used for food. Suddenly, they had no meat, no eggs, no milk. And they had no animals for breeding to create more.

"Everyone, calm down," Zakai said, and then he gave instructions for one of the ministers to check the village's coffers and see how much money they had. He then ordered two of his men to take the money and travel to another village to trade for more livestock. The people were calmed for the moment, so Zakai called his ministers, his mother, the shaman, and me into his hut to discuss what to do next. The shaman helped translate for me.

"Thankfully, we should have enough money to rebuild what we have lost," Zakai said. "Things will be lean for a time, but we can overcome this loss."

"For now," one of the ministers said. "But what if that sorceress comes back? We could spend all of our money on new animals just for her to return and slaughter those as well. Then we will have no food and no money!"

The other ministers uttered their agreement, some of them looking at me angrily. Unfortunately, they were right.

"Or what if she sends birds to eat our crops?" someone else asked.

"Or a plague!" another person cried.

My heart constricted. Keket had just ravaged their livestock. Her power was limitless. The Anwe people were in danger. Keket was coming for me. And if the Anwe stood in her way, she would decimate them. I had to leave. For everyone's safety, I couldn't stay here. I turned and headed for the door, but the shaman stood in my path.

"Move," I said. "I need to leave in order for everyone else to be safe."

"I don't agree," the shaman said.

"Are you crazy?" one of the ministers said. "Let her go! It's she who Keket wants. Why should we die for her?"

"Because Keket will not stop with Sanura," Tabia said. "Sanura is only the beginning."

"If Sanura leaves now," Zakai said, "we might buy some time for ourselves. But Keket *will* come for us."

My heart swelled. Even after the horrible way I acted, Zakai, Tabia, and the shaman were supporting me. Protecting me. Like one of their own.

"Fine," one of the ministers said. "Stay or go, what does it matter? But what will we do? With or without Sanura, how will we fight this sorceress?"

"Only by the strength of the lion kings can we defeat an enemy as powerful as Keket," the shaman said.

Everyone groaned and shook their heads—even me.

"We tried that," I said. "The kings would not listen. Oringo and Saleem simply cannot see past their differences."

"That was before Keket killed our livestock," the shaman said. "Before, Keket was a vague threat. Something that might or might not come far into the future. But now we know that she has the power to decimate a tribe in moments. The threat is here. The threat is now."

"So, do we call them back?" I asked. "Try again?"

Zakai stood from his throne and approached me. He gripped my arms and kissed my forehead. The shaman handed him a short wooden scepter, the head of which was carved like a lion. Zakai handed it to me.

"You must go to see the Dakari and the Nuru yourself," he said. "On their own turf. Meet with them as equals with my complete authority, as my emissary. Force them to see the danger we all face. Do whatever you must to broker a treaty with them. You must form an alliance."

My hands shook as I accepted the scepter from him. Even when my own father named me queen I did not feel as honored as I did now. The Anwe tribe—people who were strangers to me only weeks ago—were entrusting their lives to me.

I could not fail them.

I bowed to Zakai. "I will do as you ask, Your Majesty."

Zakai led the way out of the tent and addressed the people.

"I know you are afraid," he said. "This is an adversary the likes of which we have never faced. But as always, if we are strong, if we are united, we will prevail. We are the descendants of the Lion Queen!"

The people cheered, and I could feel a wave of optimism wash over me. Zakai took my hand and led me to the healing hut.

"Take whatever you need," he said. I nodded and went inside. I gasped when I saw that the altar had been rebuilt, the three lion skulls once again in their rightful places. I froze for a moment, not wanting to insult the sacred space. But then I decided that there was no better time to make amends with Sekhmet. Once again, I gathered candles, crystals, and herbs. I placed the crystals around the skulls and lit the candles. I cleansed the space with smoke from the herbs. I then cut my hand and dripped my blood on the skulls. I knelt before the altar, knocking my forehead to the ground.

"Goddess Sekhmet, warrior, healer, mother. Hear my plea and accept my apology. For the rest of my life, I will not cease honoring you. I swear it."

The candles flickered, but I did not feel the surge of power as I did before. Clearly, it would take some time for Sekhmet to forgive me. But as I stood, my hand healed, and I knew that she would not stay angry with me forever.

I gathered clothes, fruits and vegetables, and my khopesh. I also took my gold jewelry, wrapped in a small bag. I had nothing else to take with me. When I exited the tent, Tabia approached me and placed a small pouch around my neck. I held it to my nose and could smell the fragrant herbs inside of it.

"Mother says it is a protection charm," Zakai explained. "She says you should wear it always."

"I will," I said. I gave the pouch a squeeze and then gave Tabia a long hug. She hugged me tightly back and I knew that things were mended between us.

When I finally pulled away, the shaman sprinkled some red dust over my head before chanting some words and then drew a symbol on my forehead.

"For strength and endurance," he said, and I could almost swear I felt more energetic. More optimistic about my quest.

Zakai took my hand and led me to the edge of the village. I looked behind me and saw that most of the villagers seemed to have turned out to see me off. One of the ministers who had left to trade with the other villages returned with a horse. The nearest village must not have been far off. He handed me the reins to the horse with a bow. I mumbled my thanks, too overwhelmed with emotions to speak clearly.

Zakai sighed as he took my hands in his. "You can do this," he said.

I nodded and said, "I know," even though I wasn't sure at all I could. I wanted to believe that Oringo and Saleem would come to see reason and join with us, but that was on them. Not me. Could I really help them overcome centuries of division and come together to help me? I didn't know, but I had to have faith that I could.

Zakai hugged me and spoke into my hair. "I love you, Sanura."

"I love you too," I finally admitted.

"Come back to me," he said so softly I was not sure I heard him at first.

I looked deep into his eyes and saw something I had not seen there before—fear. I touched his face and then kissed his lips.

"I swear it," I said.

We finally forced ourselves to part and Zakai helped me mount the horse. I turned it away from Anwe village and headed deeper into Africa.

I would get my alliance or die trying.

THANK YOU FOR READING!

We hope you enjoyed The Lioness of Egypt. Don't miss
Book Two in the Shifters of Africa Trilogy,
The Pride of Egypt!
Be sure to sign up for our mailing lists so you never miss a
new release!

Leigh Anderson
http://leighandersonromance.com/subscribe/
Alice Wilde
http://alicewilde.com

THE PRIDE OF EGYPT

THE SHIFTERS OF AFRICA - BOOK 2

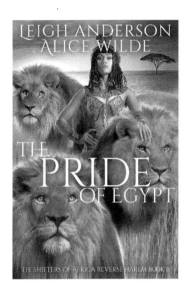

https://books2read.com/u/3LgXyJ

An ancient prophecy. A blood feud. And a heart-wrenching betrayal.

Sanura will do whatever she must to return to Egypt, save her brother, and become queen. But three lion shifter kings stand in her way. She can only succeed with an army at her back – but the men she needs can't stand the sight of one another.

One by one, Sanura must convince the lion kings to help her. And she just might lose her heart in the process...

ABOUT LEIGH ANDERSON

Leigh Anderson loves all things Gothic and paranormal. She did her master's thesis on vampire imagery in Gothic novels and met her husband while assuming the role of a vampire online. She currently teaches writing at several universities and has a rather impressive collection of tiny hats. She lives in a small town in the mountains where she raises bearded dragons and gives them wings for Halloween. She is currently working on too many writing projects, and yet not enough.

Sign up for her mailing list and stalk her around the web to keep in touch and be the first to learn about new releases. LeighAndersonRomance.com

ABOUT ALICE WILDE

 Alice Wilde grew up with a love of reading and spent her teens writing and submitting her essays as fantasy stories, much to the annoyance, but often high marks, of her teachers. Now, she spends much of her days writing historical fantasy paranormal romances (filled with gorgeous men and, of course, magic) that she hopes will spark a flame in readers as much as they do in herself.

Alice is currently living with her cat in a bustling city she never sees much of, as she's too busy dreaming up, writing down, and living in her next paranormal RH romance, though she generally finds enough time for a real-life date or two... We all need a bit of inspiration now and again, right?

SIGN UP FOR NEW RELEASE ANNOUNCEMENTS at http://alicewilde.com

facebook.com/AliceWildeAuthor

instagram.com/alice_wilde_author

bookbub.com/authors/alice-wilde

goodreads.com/alicewilde

ABOUT THE PUBLISHER

VISIT OUR WEBSITE
TO SEE ALL OF OUR HIGH QUALITY BOOKS:

http://www.redempresspublishing.com

Quality trade paperbacks, downloads, audio books, and books
in foreign languages in genres such as historical, romance,
mystery, and fantasy.

Made in the USA
Middletown, DE
15 June 2023

32589635R00109